"I've missed you," she whispered.

Arching her back, she pressed her body even closer to his. "I didn't want to, but I did."

Gavin nibbled a sensitive spot beneath her ear, making her squirm. "Why didn't you want to miss me?"

"I had plans to take over the world. To be somebody. You were a temptation I had to resist."

He knew the feeling.

Worse, now that he had tasted her again, he hadn't a snowball's chance in hell of pretending he didn't want her. One look at her sweet face and mischievous eyes and he was a goner.

He thought of the babies in her womb...and their mother.

Cassidy Corelli troubled him. He was vulnerable where she was concerned. And vulnerability was the enemy of control.

If he was going to navigate these next few weeks, then he had to stay away from her. No touching, no kissing and certainly no sex. He would make that very clear.

Convincing Cassidy was one thing. Convincing himself was going to be a whole lot more difficult.

* * *

Twins on the Way
is part of the Kavanaghs of Silver Glen series:
In the mountains of North Carolina, one family
discovers that wealth means nothing without love.

TWINS ON THE WAY

BY
JANICE MAYNARD

Published in Great Britain 2015
by Mills & Boon, an imprint of Harlequin (UK) Limited,
Eton House, 18-24 Paradise Road, Richmond, Surrey, TW9 1SR

© 2015 Janice Maynard

ISBN: 978-0-263-25786-1

Harlequin (UK) Limited's policy is to use papers that are natural, renewable and recyclable products and made from wood grown in sustainable forests. The logging and manufacturing processes conform to the legal environmental regulations of the country of origin.

Printed and bound in Great Britain
by CPI Antony Rowe, Chippenham, Wiltshire

B000 000 014 9175

Janice Maynard is a *USA TODAY* bestselling author who lives in beautiful east Tennessee with her husband. She holds a BA from Emory and Henry College and an MA from East Tennessee State University. In 2002 Janice left a fifteen-year career as an elementary school teacher to pursue writing full time. Now her first love is creating sexy, character-driven, contemporary romance stories.

Janice loves to travel and enjoys using those experiences as settings for books. Hearing from readers is one of the best perks of the job! Visit her website, www.janicemaynard.com, and follow her on Facebook and Twitter.

One

Gavin Kavanagh needed a woman. Badly. He wasn't very good at relationships. He was too damn selfish, and he had trust issues. Which meant his only choices for sexual satisfaction were typically one-night stands. Since he was too fastidious to find much pleasure in that, he usually endured months of self-imposed celibacy until the day or the week he finally decided he couldn't stand it anymore, and he cracked.

This time, what tipped him over the edge was being in Vegas. He'd pitched in at the last minute to help out a sick friend by giving an address to several thousand cyber-security experts. Though public speaking didn't bother him, he much preferred to be alone in his man cave back in North Carolina.

Winding his way past noisy slot machines and crowded gaming tables, he headed for the exit, desperate to inhale fresh air and see the sky. He'd been incarcerated in this over-the-top hotel since lunchtime, and it was now almost ten at night.

On the sidewalk, he paused, taking in the garish display of neon and traffic spread before him. Vegas. Land of opportunity and lost dreams. Home of wild bachelor parties, just-past-prime entertainers and the siren lure of the *big win*.

He could see the appeal. The outrageous city pulsed with an almost tangible energy. If New York was the city that never slept, then Las Vegas was its manic twin. With enough disposable income and plenty of unencumbered time, a man could entertain himself here indefinitely.

But not Gavin Kavanagh. He couldn't wait to go home.

Good lord, Kavanagh. Bullshitting himself was a new low.

It wasn't entirely a lie. He *did* want to go home. But there was something else he wanted more. The need writhing inside him was a voracious beast, reminding him that he was smack-dab in the land of legal hookers. For a few hundred bucks, the primeval urge to mate with a woman could be appeased.

He wasn't going to do it. What kind of man had to pay for sex? Maybe one who was too much of a curmudgeon to play nice with a decent female? To compliment her dress and ask about her day?

If that was the cost of sex as normal people enjoyed, he was out of luck. Pressing his fingertips to his temples, he winced as a shard of pain lanced its way through his head. He'd been up since 3:00 a.m. to catch a flight out of Asheville. Hell, even with a hooker, he might fall asleep before he could take care of business.

Heaving a sigh, he strode off down the street, trying to avoid looking at scantily clad women and signs for "adult" clubs. It was like putting an alcoholic in the middle of a distillery tour.

Weaving his way among tourists and time-share hawkers, he marveled that no one batted an eye at the occasional eccentrically dressed pedestrian. Perhaps Gavin was the oddity tonight.

He walked swiftly, needing the exercise to clear his head and regain control of his libido. It was almost one in the morning back home in Silver Glen. Exhaustion made him weave on his feet, but he knew he wouldn't sleep unless he was tired to the bone, not as buzzed as he was by the craving to feel a woman's soft skin and curves.

If he had his way, he'd be able to sublimate his sexual desires. He was a loner. Which meant that women either thought they could change him or were a little scared of him.

As the middle child of seven brothers, he had learned to be self-sufficient at an early age. He'd viewed his younger brothers as babies and wanted to avoid their company. His older brothers had been far too cool to tolerate little Gavin hanging around.

Even the community had unwittingly isolated Gavin. The Kavanagh brood had been referred to as the Three Musketeers—Liam, Dylan and Aidan...and the Three Stooges—Conor, Patrick and James. Gavin was often overlooked, partly because he didn't make waves.

He liked school. He never got in trouble. And though he grew to six feet in height by the ninth grade and two years later had filled out his gangly frame with muscles, he was often found with his head in a book. He knew how to fight. He could hold his own in a brawl.

But why do that when there were so many more interesting ways to spend his time?

He cut down a side street and followed it several blocks. Then, reversing his original course, he headed toward the hotel. Back here, away from the strip, there were not as many streetlights...less activity...fewer temptations to do something he might regret later. Unfortunately, he was not the only one to choose this route.

As he drew even with an alley that accommodated delivery trucks, he overheard a heated exchange. Pausing just out of sight, he listened.

The female voice surprised him. This was no place for a woman. She made her displeasure clear. "Leave me alone," she cried. "You can't have everything your way."

Gavin peeked around the corner just as the man put his hands on the woman's shoulders and shook her. The guy was about twice her size. "Stay out of it, Cass," he said. "Or you'll be sorry."

That was enough for Gavin. Hurling himself into the alley, he shouted, "Let go of her."

The petite dark-haired woman struggled, but the man had her wrists now, holding her hands away from his body. Gavin's yell distracted the guy for a split second, enabling the woman to land a blow.

"*Ow*, damn it."

Gavin seized the opportunity. With one efficient upper-cut to the chin, he caused the bully to stagger backward. The guy was huge and wouldn't have fallen, but his foot slid in loose gravel. He lost his balance and went down hard, his shoulder striking the ground first. He didn't move.

"Hurry," Gavin said, taking the woman's arm and dragging her behind him. "We don't want to be here when he wakes up."

"But what if he's hurt?"

Gavin paused beneath a security light to examine her face with incredulity. "Do you really care?"

Big dark eyes framed in impossibly long lashes stared at him. Small white teeth worried a lower lip that was plump and shiny. "I suppose not," she said quietly. But she glanced over her shoulder nevertheless.

She was not the kind of woman Gavin needed tonight. Innocence framed her in an almost visible aura. His gut responded to that innocence on a visceral level with cave-man lust, but he wanted sex that was hard and fast and insane. This sweet young thing was not in his league. He would scare her to death.

Still…he couldn't resist the urge to touch her. Tucking her hair behind her ear, he brushed her cheek with his thumb. "You're okay," he said. "I won't let anything happen to you, I swear."

Her gaze clashed with his. He felt as if he knew her somehow, a strange sense of déjà vu as if he had dreamed this moment before.

"You're very kind," she said.

"No. I'm not. But I don't like men who use their size to threaten women." He could have stood there looking at her all night. She made him feel things that confused him. Aroused him.

Dragging his concentration back to the matter at hand, he touched her arm. "We should go now." He urged her along, glad to see that even wearing four-inch heels, she was able to keep up with him. She kept a death grip on the small purse slung over her shoulder. "My car is parked at the hotel," he said. "I can give you a ride home."

"No." The negative was forceful. "He knows where I live."

Hell's bells. "Okay, then. But we need to call the police. You should make a formal complaint."

It was difficult to carry on a conversation when both parties were almost running. And perhaps speed was no longer called for, because there was no sign they were being followed.

"My side hurts," she complained. "And I don't want to involve the police."

Slowing reluctantly, he exhaled as she leaned against a mailbox, her chest heaving.

He tried not to notice her breasts.

"How much farther?" she asked.

He named the hotel in the next block. "Did he hurt you?" Though the man's threat had sounded menacing, Gavin hadn't seen the guy do more than shake the woman, though that was bad enough. The argument had been escalating, however, so no telling what would have happened if Gavin hadn't been around to stop it.

The woman straightened. "I'm fine." Her steady gaze took him in with a head-to-toe inspection that made him mildly uncomfortable. "You could take me to your room," she said. "So I can calm down and catch my breath."

Gavin froze, his nostrils flaring as if he could actually inhale her scent like a wild animal recognizing its mate. "I don't know if that's wise." Was this some kind of sick cosmic test of his character?

"I won't bother you. Unless you want me to," she said with a quick mischievous grin. "But I don't want to be alone right now. Please."

God help him, there was sexual interest in those beautiful eyes. He cleared his throat. "If that's what you want. Let's go."

This time, as Gavin traversed the acres of gaming floor in his hotel, he barely noticed the crowd. All his focus was on the woman he had rescued. He held her narrow wrist in one hand, sure he could feel the blood pulsing in her veins as he threaded his way through the throng, pulling her behind him. In the elevator he finally had a chance to see her clearly.

While she stared at the carpeted floor, he studied her, his heart thudding, his muscles jerky with leftover adrenaline. Chin-length curly hair somewhere between dark brown and black framed a heart-shaped face. Though she couldn't be more than five foot four at most, she appeared taller thanks to the outrageous shoes.

God, he loved those shoes. He could see her wearing nothing *but* those shoes as he laid her out on his big soft bed.

Down, boy. He told himself he wouldn't take advantage of her vulnerable state. But he had lied to himself once tonight already.

She was rounded in all the right places, including generous breasts that threatened to spill out of the neckline of her low-cut silver dress. The material was some kind of metallic fabric that sparkled when the lights hit it. Every time she moved, the dress moved with her.

Gavin reeled from the punch of sexual hunger. Any woman would have affected him the same, he told himself. She was nothing special. "What's your name?" he asked.

When she lifted her head and smiled, the hunger intensified. "Cassidy. Cassidy Corelli. My friends call me Cass. And who are you?"

"Gavin Kavanagh."

The elevator dinged. Together, they stepped out. Gavin's room was down the hallway and around the corner. He inserted the key card, opened the door and stood back for his guest to enter.

Cassidy surveyed the plush suite with raised eyebrows. "You're either a high roller or somebody very important."

"Not exactly." He sprawled in an armchair, trying to appear relaxed. It was probably not a good idea to let her see the beast that rode him. "I don't gamble. My friend was supposed to do the keynote at a conference here, but he got sick. I'm subbing."

Casually, as if it were the most normal thing in the world, Cassidy slipped off her shoes and went to the minibar. Without waiting for permission, she extracted a soft drink and a jar of macadamia nuts. "Do you mind? I missed dinner, and I'm starving."

"Help yourself." When she took the chair opposite his,

he nearly swallowed his tongue. The skirt of her dress was unforgiving. As she curled her legs beneath her, he caught a glimpse of bare thighs all the way to the mother lode.

He swallowed hard. "Do you have a phone, or do you need to use mine?"

She took a swig of soda, managing to look entirely comfortable and yet ladylike. "Why do I need a phone?"

"To call the authorities?" Her artless stonewalling scraped his nerves. Was she deliberately tormenting him?

Cassidy wrinkled her small, perfect nose. "I'm not sure that would be a good idea. This is sort of a family squabble."

His gut tightened. "As in the mob?"

Her jaw dropped. "Good grief, no."

"Are you married to the guy?" She wasn't wearing a ring, but that didn't mean anything. The scene he had interrupted could have been a domestic dispute.

Cassidy stared at him. Her lips were painted the same deep red as her toenails. "I'm not married," she said, enunciating each word carefully. "I don't have a significant other. I'm entirely unencumbered. And I don't have to be anywhere until ten in the morning."

The look she gave him tightened the back of his neck… and other body parts. Still, caution won out. "Are you a working girl?" he asked. In Vegas it could be hard to tell. Cassidy Corelli more than lived up to male fantasy, but she seemed awfully young.

She pursed her lips, suddenly looking more like a schoolmarm than a woman for hire. "I *work*," she muttered, glaring at him. "But not like that. I don't know whether to be insulted or flattered."

"How old are you?" In other circumstances, he would never ask such personal questions, but he also didn't want to contribute to the delinquency of a minor.

"I'm twenty-three," she said flatly, erasing most of his misgivings.

"Good."

She cocked her head. "Why is that good?"

He gave her a gentle smile. "Because if I follow up on your invitation, I want to make sure I don't end up in jail."

"What invitation?" she asked, feigning innocence, though in those huge expressive eyes, feminine excitement lingered.

His customary distrust of unknown women cautioned him to slow down. But Cassidy was light and warmth and spontaneity, all the things that were missing from his life. He was irresistibly drawn to her vibrant personality like the proverbial moth to a flame. But he'd been burned once…badly. So the doubts remained.

"Don't be coy. A woman doesn't outline her relationship status quite so succinctly unless she wants a man to know the score."

"Ah." Cassidy popped a nut into her mouth and chewed it slowly before swallowing and taking another sip of her drink. "Why don't you gamble?" she asked.

The non sequitur caught him off guard. He shrugged. "I'm good at math. But the house always wins. I prefer to control the outcome."

She gave a mock shiver. "So intense. I like that in a man."

"Is that why you were hanging around with Bozo the Bruiser?"

"Trust me," she said. "There's nothing romantic there."

"What were you arguing about?"

"I'd rather not discuss it."

"You're willing to have sex with a stranger, but you won't answer a simple question?"

She tossed her head and stood up, cheeks flushing. "Who said I'm willing to have sex?"

He gazed at her intently, letting her see the arousal that had built since he looked her over in the elevator. "No games, Cass. You tossed out a pretty blatant lure. Stay or go. Your choice."

Cassidy shivered inwardly. Gavin Kavanagh was a man, not a boy. He'd rescued her from what he thought was a dangerous situation, not pausing to consider the consequences. Though she was more than capable of taking care of herself, Gavin's masculine assurance triggered all sorts of non-PC feminine emotions.

He was a beautiful man. Tall and broad…exuding confidence. The combination made her damp in places she'd rather not ponder. His streaky brownish-blond hair was short and spiky, not expertly styled, but like a man who didn't care to fool with anything he considered a waste of time.

His gray eyes with the hint of blue were cool and distant at the moment. "Which is it?" The question was rife with masculine demand.

"Grumpy, grumpy, grumpy." She wanted more time to think about this, but if she let the moment pass, she would never see him again. She was tired of being her father's good little girl. Everyone expected her to live like a nun. And she had. But why? Her whole life was about work, work, work, and earning the love that should be a gift.

She'd been edgy and stressed for weeks now, arguing with her brother and going head-to-head with her father. Perhaps if she'd had a mother, she could have talked frankly about the fact that she felt like the world's oldest virgin. About her choice to wait for the right man. And the fact that she'd never even met a guy who honestly tempted her.

Being raised in Vegas had exposed her to a whole lot of mature situations that gave her an insight into all kinds of adult behavior. But it also took some of the bloom off the rose when it came to romance. She was probably holding out for a fantasy that didn't even exist except in books and movies.

She took a deep breath, feeling a funny spin in the pit of her stomach. To hell with her status as the firstborn who never strayed from the straight and narrow. She could blame Gavin for her sexual epiphany, but truthfully, this moment had been coming for a long time. She'd been saving herself for some unknown white knight, but surprisingly, the tarnished armor of a gruff, no-nonsense, make-my-day kind of guy punched all her buttons.

Though it took a measure of courage and nonchalance she wasn't sure she could pull off, she went to him and perched on his lap, curling one arm around his neck. "You could kiss me. It might help me make up my mind."

A firm hand gripped her hip. He smelled amazing. Woodsy cologne and warm male skin. She wanted things from him. Wild things. Wicked things. And that was saying a lot for a girl who had grown up in sin city.

"I should toss you out on your butt," he muttered. "You're a menace to the male sex."

"Really?" Could he be telling the truth?

"You're playing a dangerous game."

The suspicion in his hard eyes was perhaps warranted, but it stung. "Don't be that way," she said. Putting a hand to his stubbly cheek, she smiled wistfully. "I'll go if you want me to. But I'd really like to stay."

He made her wait a miserably long time. Maybe thirty seconds. Or more. She actually *felt* the moment she won the standoff. Though she was technically on top, Gavin took control right out of the gate. One big hand settled in the curls at the back of her head, pulling her down until his lips could reach hers.

"Gavin…" She had no idea what she meant to say. When his mouth settled over hers, her brain short-circuited. He was a great kisser. World-class. On a scale of one to ten, a thirteen. The only unlucky thing about that number was that they were both fully dressed.

He took his time, drawing attention to the fact that her experience was limited at best. Unapologetic, he slid his tongue into her mouth, mimicking the act they both wanted.

When she was starved for oxygen, he pulled back, his heavy-lidded gaze searching hers. "I don't know why you're here," he said gruffly, with perhaps the slightest note of accusation in his voice.

"I can leave." It would probably be best if she did. What had started as a personal declaration of independence suddenly seemed far more serious.

"Do you do this often?"

The insinuation infuriated her. "No," she snapped. "How about you?"

He grinned. "Never. Maybe we're experiencing Vegas madness. I've heard about it."

"I wouldn't know," she sniffed. "I'm a native."

"And I'm a novice."

"You're not a *novice* anything," she said drily. "But I could show you the sights if you're interested."

"I fly home tomorrow."

"We have tonight." She was skating a fine line between taking what she wanted and being totally reckless. But after four years of college and two years of grad school without a break, she wanted to know how it felt to be a woman. In every way.

He toyed with the neckline of her dress. The feel of his slightly rough fingertips on her bare skin made her nipples pebble. "The only sights I'm interested in at the moment are in this room."

The words were flat. Unadorned with emotion. The blaze in his eyes more than made up for it. So much so that she almost chickened out. To him, she had been a damsel in distress. He had acted honorably, protecting her from a perceived enemy. Only a man with high moral standards did that…right?

She'd always been a good judge of character. It was a necessary skill growing up in Vegas, particularly when your family had a lot of money. Every gut instinct she possessed told her that Gavin Kavanagh was one of the good guys. He was leaving in the morning. Was there any point in starting something that would never amount to anything more?

Playing by the rules was a first-child burden. Good grades, never breaking curfew, always trying to satisfy the parental units. Tonight she was damned if she was going to miss out on something incredible because she was too afraid to take a walk on the wild side.

"I'd like to take a shower." The follow-up didn't need to be spelled out.

"May I join you?"

So polite. But it wasn't really a question. She swallowed hard. "I suppose."

He shifted her out of his lap onto her feet. Her legs felt like overcooked pasta and her heartbeat was none too steady.

"I like your hair." He ruffled his hand through it, mussing the style.

Every time she thought she had him pinned down, he surprised her. Men in general had little patience when it came to sexual gratification. At least the ones she knew. Gavin, on the other hand, possessed remarkable restraint.

"Thank you," she said.

"Don't get shy now." He chuckled, taking her hand and leading her across the thick carpet that made her toes curl.

The bathroom was palatial and decadent. She spared a glance for the hot tub, but Gavin shook his head. "Later."

He turned the faucet control in the glass enclosure. Triple showerheads sprouted streams of water. "Last chance."

They were both still fully clothed except for her shoes. Though he might not like it, she knew she could turn around and leave the suite. He wouldn't chase after her. Her confidence wavered. Was she really about to get stark naked with a handsome stranger in his opulent shower stall?

She spared a glance in the mirror, hardly recognizing the woman who stood there. "Do you have any wine?"

"Needing a bit of Dutch courage, are we?"

"Don't make fun of me," she said. "You're an intimidating man."

"Which is why you insisted on coming to my room and throwing yourself at me."

Hot color swept from her throat to her hairline. From where he was standing, it must have seemed that way. How could she explain that he had dazzled her without even trying? "You'll be disappointed if you think I'm a pro."

"I thought we already established that you're *not* a pro."

"That's not what I mean. I haven't *done* this kind of thing."

"Sex? Or seduction?"

"I have not seduced you," she said primly, secretly charmed that he thought she could.

He nodded briefly, his firm lips curved in a sensual smile. "I'll admit to being predisposed. You're a very appealing woman."

The die was cast. "How about fetching us some of that wine while I get undressed?"

Two

Gavin's hands shook as he opened a bottle of Zinfandel. He managed to pour two glasses without spilling anything, but it was a close call. In his bathroom was a naked young female…the most beautiful woman he had seen in a very long time. If he had to create a sexual partner from scratch, she would look a lot like Cassidy Corelli.

Her sun-kissed Mediterranean coloring and cheeky personality were irresistible. He'd never particularly believed in fate as the arbiter of his destiny. He was too much of a control freak for that. But some unseen force or quirk of timing had put him near that alley at exactly the right moment. It was his choice how to proceed.

He carried the wine into the bathroom and stopped dead in his tracks when he realized that Cassidy was already undressed. She had donned one of the hotel's signature bathrobes. It was much too large for her.

"Most people wait until *after* the shower to cover up," he said drily. The acres of terry cloth might as well have been armor. But what his guest didn't realize was that bare feet and flushed cheeks gave her an air of innocence. The juxtaposition of smart-mouthed banter with youthful naïveté brought tenderness into the mix.

"I was cold," she said.

Since the bathroom was steamy, he took that with a

grain of salt. Though he had turned off the water when he saw they weren't getting in immediately, the room was plenty warm.

"Drink some wine," he said, handing her a glass. "It will settle your nerves."

She scowled at him over the rim of her crystal flute. "Who says I'm nervous?"

Leaning a hip against the counter, he drained half his glass. "Aren't you? Shouldn't you be?"

"Not unless you're a twisted psychopath."

"It's a little late to worry about that now, don't you think?"

She set down the glass of wine she had barely touched and shoved her hands in her pockets. Her chin lifted. "I can read people."

"Do tell."

"You were a Boy Scout. Eagle, if I had to guess."

He lifted an eyebrow. "I'm impressed."

"So I'm right?" Her pleased smugness amused him.

"One lucky shot doesn't qualify you to read the Tarot cards."

"I don't need cards. You're an open book."

He emptied his glass and set it gently on the counter with a little *clink*. "Then what am I thinking now?" He unfastened his belt and drew it from around his waist. When he dropped it on the floor, he was pretty sure she gulped.

"Stop that," she said.

"I seldom shower with my clothes on." His solemn joke lightened the look of panic on her face, though she still eyed him warily.

"Maybe we should get to know each other first."

"Did I mention that I'm flying out in the morning? Leave if you want to, Cass, but soon. I don't want to go any further with this if you aren't sure."

She paled, her brown eyes round with a mix of emotions he couldn't decipher. "I *want* to be sure."

"But you're not," he said, reading her fairly well.

"I thought I could be spontaneous and adventuresome. But it turns out I'm not really that girl."

He swallowed his disappointment. "I understand. Get dressed and I'll take you wherever you want to go."

She took a step in his direction, placing her small hand on his forearm. "How about a compromise?"

It became painfully clear that Cassidy Corelli didn't know much about men at all. She was naked for all intents and purposes, in his bathroom, and yet somehow she expected him to play nice. Even her fingers on his skin made him shudder with hunger.

Moving out of reach, he ran two hands through his hair. "What kind of compromise?" He was asking for more physical torture, but he didn't have it in him to kick her out.

"This is your first trip to Vegas, right?"

"Yes."

"I could show you the sights for a couple of hours. Enjoy the ambiance."

"And then what?"

"Whatever we want to do next."

Her smile seemed genuine. Was she deliberately teasing him, or did she honestly want to go to bed with him but was uncertain about the wisdom of that plan?

He was hard and ready. It wasn't conceit to think he could coax her into having sex right now. But he'd been raised to be a gentleman. Despite the demands of his body, he was well aware that Cassidy was not 100 percent on board with the idea of intimacy. Even if she *had* been the one to come on to him in the first place.

The smart thing for both of them would be for him to boot her out before somebody got hurt. He couldn't give her anything beyond tonight. And it was pretty clear that she was not a woman who went in for casual sex.

But she fascinated him, intrigued him…and he couldn't remember ever wanting a woman more. He was not in the habit of picking up strange females, especially not ones like Cassidy. Too many unknowns. Too many warning bells.

He'd learned the hard way not to be taken in by a seemingly innocent come-on. Cassidy was more than that, though. He believed it, or told himself he did. Otherwise, he was about to break his personal code into tiny unmanageable pieces.

His desire for her and her undeniable appeal could be blamed on Vegas, but whatever compelled him was strong and urgent.

"Fine," he said tersely. "Put your clothes on, and we'll see the sights." He'd been awake for almost twenty-four hours, but what the hell. Carpe diem it was…God help him.

When they reached Gavin's rental car, Cassidy was delighted to see it was a convertible. "Why don't I drive so you can enjoy yourself?" she said.

Gavin yawned and nodded. "Probably a good idea. I'm sleep-deprived." He went around to the passenger side. "You're in charge."

She didn't think he meant that statement to be provocative, but the image it conjured made her shift restlessly as she settled behind the wheel. Gavin Kavanagh was an imposing man. Imagining him nude and at her mercy made her mouth dry and her cheeks hot.

Once they folded back the top and exited the parking garage, her passenger slumped in his seat with his head against the headrest. She drove down the strip, pointing out places of interest that were unique to Vegas. The fabulous architecture, the neon lights, the endless spectacle and the marquees touting famous entertainers.

When she paused at a traffic light, Gavin waved a hand. "You love it here, don't you?"

His perception surprised her. "I suppose I do. We take the good with the bad. There's nothing like it anywhere in the world."

"I wasn't too impressed with Vegas before tonight. You've convinced me it has a lot to offer."

When she glanced sideways at him, the look in his eyes made her shiver. He wanted her. And he planned to have her.

Sweet heaven. Without asking, she turned the car around and headed out of town. She barely remembered her name. Sexual arousal flooded her veins, hot and sweet. Exhilaration, laced with anticipation, made her feel as if she could fly.

Fortunately, gravity kept her grounded. Driving in the desert at night was a special pleasure. The road was straight, traffic sparse and the spring air invigorating.

She was a good driver, and she knew her limits. Pressing down on the gas, she watched the speedometer hit sixty, then seventy, then eighty. In her peripheral vision, she saw Gavin straighten. "I'm not paying for any tickets," he said.

The implied but laconic warning made her grin. She pushed it to ninety and laughed out loud as the wind tangled her hair. "Don't worry. I know every law enforcement official in a fifty-mile radius." She had to raise her voice for him to hear her.

A rush of adrenaline took over, encompassing an odd mix of sexual hunger and sheer fun. Her hands were steady on the wheel. Anticipation rose in her chest like a wave of bubbles. The night was hers...the open road, as well. Earlier, she had panicked, plain and simple. She had second-guessed her decision to change the status quo. But now she was ready. She wanted Gavin Kavanagh, and she wasn't going to let her inexperience stand in her way.

Only the late hour curtailed her road trip. At last, she eased off on the accelerator and dropped back to a more sedate speed. At a pullout on the right, she slid the car to a stop and turned off the engine. The sudden silence was deafening. Overhead, a million stars twinkled and sparked.

Gavin reached for her before she had a chance to take her hands off the wheel. His kiss was urgent. Thorough. Masterful. She had assumed he was half-asleep. Which proved how wrong a woman could be. This was a hunger that had been building since she went to his hotel room.

The kiss was firm and demanding. It sent little squiggles of lust into every cell of her body. His hands anchored her head, one on each side of her jaw. Tilting her face to his, he ravaged her mouth, barely giving her a moment to breathe.

For Cassidy, it was earth-shattering. She'd never been too impressed with foreplay. In the course of her limited experimentation, it had proven to be awkward and usually disappointing. Apparently her subconscious had recognized Gavin Kavanagh as the man to prove her wrong.

Desperately, she pondered the logistics of getting naked in the backseat. But while she didn't mind being pulled over for speeding, getting caught in sexual flagrante delicto was another matter entirely. This was Vegas, true. But her father would have a coronary, and this was not a time she wanted to court his displeasure.

Gavin had more control than she did, apparently. He eventually gentled the kiss and released her, though his chest heaved. "You dazzle me, Cassidy Corelli."

His rough praise stroked her ego. Coming from a man

like Gavin, that was a compliment worth savoring. "The feeling is mutual."

He snorted. "You sound like a little girl practicing her social etiquette. Tell me honestly. Why are you here in this car with me?"

"I really don't know," she said, recognizing the truth as she spoke it. "But I never had a choice. There's something about you I can't resist." She paused, grimacing. "We get lots of flimflam artists in Vegas. Con men, gaming sharks, wannabe Don Juans. So I've learned how to spot them. But you're different, Gavin Kavanagh. You're the real deal. Don't ask me how I know. I just do…"

He leaned back in his seat with a sigh, but he took her hand in his. "This is the first time all day I've felt comfortable. The stars are just as bright in North Carolina."

His thumb played lightly over the pulse point at the back of her wrist, making her dizzy. "Do you live at the beach?" she asked.

"No. In a place called Silver Glen. It's in the western part of the state…in the mountains. My ancestors discovered a silver mine back in the day and restored the family fortunes after the Depression." He pointed to a group of stars. "Do you know your astronomy? Those are the Pleiades…the seven sisters. And over there is Orion. The fuzzy spot in his dagger is a nebula."

"You're very smart, aren't you?"

He chuckled. "Any third grader worth his salt can spot those."

She half turned in her seat, forcing him to release her hand. She couldn't see his expression very well. "There's one more place I need to go, just a quick stop, and then I'd very much like to return to your hotel. For real this time. You know…to—"

He put a hand over her mouth. "Don't say it out loud. I'm on a hair trigger. But I'm trying to behave myself."

A sudden gust of wind made her shiver. At night the desert temperatures plummeted. She wanted to cuddle into the warmth of his embrace, but if she did, they might not make it back to the hotel. And while she was prepared to lose her innocence with him, she would prefer her first time to be in more traditional surroundings.

She settled for nipping his fingers with her teeth. The naughty bite drew a groan and a curse from him. He gripped her shoulders. "You're playing with fire, Cass. I'm not averse to taking you over the hood of the car. Is that what you want?"

The possibility that he might decide to do just that made her melt inside. She could see herself, spread-eagled, Gavin lifting her skirt from behind and moving against her. She felt lost in an emotional desert, desperate for water. The inside of her mouth was like sand. "No." *Yes. Yes. Yes.*

He released her and sat back in his seat. "Then let's get out of here."

Gavin wondered if she had spiked his wine somehow. He was more aroused than he could ever remember, his body trembling with the need to mate with hers. Perhaps it was the magic of this perfect night or her radiant beauty or the laughter they shared. But whatever the reason, he scarcely knew himself.

Going along with her lead was a signal of his trust, though he might be falling through a rabbit hole for the second time in his life. His hunger eradicated most of his reservations, though the wariness lurked at a subterranean level. Once they were back in sight of neon and fake waterfalls and massive pleasure palaces, it occurred to him to ask where they were going.

Cassidy gave him an impish grin. "No visit to Vegas is complete without seeing an all-night wedding chapel. My cousin is an Elvis impersonator. I want you to meet him. Besides, I promised him I'd stop by and see him tonight, because he's bored."

"Now?" It was the wee hours of the morning.

"Yeah. Robbie is being punished with the overnight shift for a few weeks. He didn't renew his license when he was supposed to, and he *married* several couples whose weddings turned out to be illegal. He almost got fired over it, but the boss has a soft spot for him, because Robbie can actually sing. So while they're waiting for his new license, he's stuck vacuuming the chapel and doing paperwork."

"What happens if a couple actually comes in wanting to get married?"

"Robbie calls the boss and wakes him up so he can dash over here." She parked the car at the curb in front of an improbably pink edifice decorated with white doves. It looked as if a bottle of Pepto-Bismol had thrown up.

"Good lord. Do people actually do this?"

Cassidy shook her head as she got out of the car. "You'd be surprised."

Inside, Robbie was visibly grateful for the company. "How's it hangin', Cass? I haven't seen you since Uncle Bobo's birthday party."

"I'm good," Cass said. "This is my friend Gavin."

Robbie appeared to be about the same age as Cass, but it was hard to tell for sure. He wore a white Elvis suit with a matching cape lined in electric-blue satin. His hair, and it looked real, was coal black with huge sideburns. "Very nice to meet you, sir."

Gavin winced inwardly. *Sir?* Did he really look that old? "Cassidy has been giving me a tour of Vegas. She said we had to stop here to make the night complete."

Cass's eyes met his. She shot him a look to which Robbie was oblivious…a look that said something entirely different would make the night complete. Gavin's brow dampened. How long could a man wait for a woman like this?

Robbie lifted a hand. "Follow me. I'll show you the Chapel of Love."

When Gavin muttered under his breath, Cass smacked his hand. "Be nice," she whispered. "This is the first job Robbie has been able to keep. We try to encourage him."

Gavin curbed his impatience as Robbie gave them the grand tour. When they stood in front of the altar, Robbie donned a white robe and stepped behind the podium. "Take her hands," he said pompously.

"Is this a shotgun wedding?" Gavin was only half kidding. But he took Cassidy's hands in his and faced her.

His faux bride frowned. "Not to worry. We don't have the paperwork. But I'm pretty sure Robbie could use the practice, if you don't mind."

Robbie grimaced. "Forgot something already." He stepped to one side and picked up a bottle of champagne. Popping the cork with a surprisingly practiced motion, he filled two flutes and handed one to Cassidy and one to Gavin.

Cassidy took a sip. "Wait a minute. Are you going to charge me for this?"

"On the house," Robbie said, snickering.

Gavin drained his drink, eager to finish whatever it took to get Cassidy back to his hotel room. When the room spun just a tad, he second-guessed the champagne.

Cass set her mostly full glass aside and took his hand again. "Go ahead, Robbie. What comes next?"

"Um…" He fumbled for his notes. "Do you, Cassidy

Lavinia Corelli, take this man to be your lawfully wedded husband?"

Gavin grinned. "Lavinia?"

His bride scowled at him. "Oh, hush." She turned to Robbie. "You're doing fine," she said. "And yes, I do."

Robbie gave Gavin a sober stare that lost something in the translation thanks to his attire. "Do you, Gavin...?" He stumbled to a halt.

"Gavin Michael Kavanagh..." Gavin felt sorry for the kid if he was really this inept when it came to his job.

"Do you, *Gavin Michael Kavanagh*, take this woman to be your lawfully wedded wife?"

For a split second, Gavin felt the earth shift beneath his feet. His brain was mush, definitely impaired thanks to lack of sleep and alcohol. But one thing was perfectly clear. If he had ever daydreamed of his wedding day—and that was something a guy definitely did not do—the woman he might have envisioned would be a clone of Cassidy Corelli.

Clearing his throat, he forgot about the late hour and the goofy Elvis and the fact that he hated Vegas. Instead, he looked into long-lashed eyes that were clear and guileless. A tiny smile played around lips curved into a perfect ruby bow. The only flaw he could see was her wind-tossed hair, and even that wasn't so bad, because it made him think of sex.

Robbie backed up and started again. "Do you, Gavin—"

Gavin held up his hand, stopping the vow prompt mid-sentence. Gripping Cassidy's fingers, he imagined what it was going to feel like when she was soft and naked in his bed. "I do," he muttered. "I definitely do. And now I'm going to kiss my bride."

Three

Cassidy had heard the term *swept off her feet*, but she had never actually experienced the phenomenon. The moment when Gavin scooped her up against his chest was both emotionally and physically exhilarating. Her heart pounded and her stomach fluttered.

It was ridiculously retro to be aroused by a man's physical strength, but damn...Gavin Kavanagh was a sexy beast. Ever since Rhett Butler carried Scarlett O'Hara up that grand staircase to have his wicked manly way with her, women had secretly judged a guy's swoon factor by how easily he could heft his lover.

Cassidy could stand to lose ten pounds. But Gavin lifted her as if she weighed no more than a child. Oh, my...

She tasted desperation in his kiss, laced with a nuance of the nice champagne. Her breasts were squished up against a hard rib cage. Kissing him back eagerly, she might have forgotten a thing or two. Like the fact that they had a witness.

Robbie moved restlessly. When she sneaked a sideways peek at him, he was slack-jawed, perhaps stunned. "I need to get back to the office," he muttered. "You two can show yourselves out."

Cassidy wiggled until Gavin released her. There was a look in his eyes that made her a little crazy. But she concentrated on her cousin. "Thanks for showing us around, Robbie."

"Thanks for stopping by to see me." He lifted a hand. "I now pronounce you husband and wife."

She hugged him and kissed his cheek. "You'll get the hang of this. Just stick with it."

Moments later, the little chapel was silent. Gavin crossed his arms over his chest and stared at her with an expression that could have meant anything.

Following an impulse, she held out her hand. "Let me have your phone. I want you to have a picture to remember me by."

She was somewhat bemused when he cooperated. Scooting up against him, she tapped a couple of icons and held the phone at arm's length. "We have to document this night."

Unfortunately, her arms were short and Gavin was tall. She couldn't actually hold the camera far enough away.

He took it out of her hand. "Give me that." With one hard arm curled around her waist and the other extended, he framed the two of them in the small screen. "Say cheese," he muttered.

Just as he hit the button, she reached up and kissed him on the chin. Afterward, she bounced on her toes. "Let me see, let me see."

The shot was surprisingly sweet. She studied Gavin's face in the image. Even if she hadn't met him in person, she would be impressed with the man in the picture. He looked like a throwback to the steely-eyed cowboys of the past. All brooding machismo and sizzling intensity. "I like it," she said. "You're very photogenic."

He lifted an eyebrow. "No. I'm not. Let's get out of here."

She followed him obediently, smothering a smile. Apparently a man like Gavin took her compliment as an affront to his masculinity. Since she had wounded his pride, she held out the car keys. "I don't have to drive."

He shook his head and slid into the passenger seat. "Yes, you do," he said, his eyelids drifting shut. "I'm taking a nap between here and the hotel so I'll have the energy to rock your world."

Laughing out loud at his tongue-in-cheek boast, she started the car. Maybe he was serious. He didn't even flinch when she whipped out into traffic. But minutes later when she eased into a spot in the parking garage, he sat up and ran a hand through his hair. "What time is it?" he asked, rubbing his eyes with the heels of his hands.

Cassidy glanced at the dashboard. "Almost four."

He grimaced. "There's something unnatural about a city where no one sleeps."

"They sleep," she protested, vaguely defensive about her hometown. "But not necessarily from midnight until morning." Though Gavin Kavanagh would never be anything other than handsome, he definitely looked the worse for wear. Dark circles beneath his eyes and a pale undertone to his skin bespoke his exhaustion. "I should go," she said impulsively, squashing her disappointment. "You need to get some rest before you fly out."

The look he gave her sizzled nerve endings in some very interesting places. "I can sleep when I'm dead," he growled. "You're not going anywhere."

The arrogance was justified given her propensity for throwing herself at him tonight. But it rankled nevertheless. "Is that a threat?"

He cupped her neck with one hand and pulled her into his kiss. "Call it what you want, Cassidy Corelli. But if I'm going to be a guinea pig in your goofy cousin's wedding charade, then I think I'm entitled to a fake honeymoon, too." He claimed her mouth with knee-weakening mastery. "C'mon, Cass. I need a bed. ASAP."

"Because you're tired?"

He got out and came around to her door, helping her to her feet. "Because I need you. Now."

Gavin had never been more serious or more desperate to have a woman. Granted, it had been several months since the last time he'd been naked with a female. In addition to his youthful catastrophic history in misjudging the fairer sex, when he lost himself in his work, his hermit leanings tended to take over. He liked people. But solitude gave him energy. Sharpened his mind. Spurred his creativity.

When it came to Cassidy, however, he was neither clear-headed nor particularly intelligent. His brain was not in the driver's seat. He wanted her. Fiercely. Madly. In a way that wiped out all his normal reservations. With an insanity no doubt induced by sleep deprivation and champagne and recent celibacy. But insanity nevertheless.

Later, he would not be able to recall the exact sequence of steps that took them from the artificially illuminated parking garage to the thickly carpeted hallway where his room was located. But through it all, he kept Cassidy by his side, hip to hip, his arm around her shoulders.

She laughed at him when he fumbled the key card from his shirt pocket and took three tries to open the door. "Are you sure this is your room?" she whispered.

The door swung wide. "Don't you remember? You were here not that long ago."

She passed him, entering the suite with a swish of hips and a low chuckle that went straight to his gut and hardened his aching sex even more. "All these hallways look alike."

The door closed with a muffled sound. For the first

time, his charming, funny tour guide seemed momentarily abashed. Her eyes wouldn't meet his. Graceful hands fluttered as if not knowing where to land.

He restrained the urge to grab her, an odd feeling in the pit of his stomach. "Problem, Cass?"

She licked her lips. "No."

The simple negative didn't sound convincing. "What's wrong?"

"Nothing." She kicked off her shoes as she had earlier, still not looking at him. "Would you mind if I take a quick shower…alone?"

He frowned, immediately suspicious. "If you think waiting will make me want you more, you're crazy. I'm far past teasing, I promise you."

Her chin came up at last and she grimaced. "I've never showered with a man. It may not seem like it, but I'm shy in certain situations. I won't linger, I swear. I want this, too."

Something about the vulnerability and honesty in her bittersweet chocolate gaze convinced him she wasn't playing games.

Nodding tersely, he put some distance between them. "Go, then."

When she disappeared, he drew in oxygen with a sharp inhale. Was Cassidy Corelli some kind of scam artist? Would he awake to find his billfold missing? Or was she what she seemed…an artless, far-too-young-for-him ingenue with a propensity for flirtation?

He paced automatically, doing everything he could think of to get himself under control. The last woman he'd slept with had been an artist in Asheville. They'd met at the home of mutual friends and acted on a quiet attraction that proved to be physically satisfying. Despite having much in common, their relationship had ended after six months due to a lack of fire.

That wasn't going to be a problem with Cassidy. Though this current encounter had all the earmarks of a one-night stand, what he felt at this pivotal moment was far more volatile than simple attraction. It wasn't that he wanted Cass. He *craved* her...with an intensity that alarmed his well-ordered existence.

Thankfully, she was true to her word. She reappeared in a very short amount of time wearing the same robe she had modeled earlier. He cleared his throat. "All done?"

She nodded, staring at him.

"Give me three minutes," he said. In the shower, he washed rapidly. The taut skin covering his erect sex was almost too sensitive to touch. Imagining Cassidy's fingers on his body made him groan.

When he stepped out of the shower, he caught his reflection in the mirror. It gave him pause. His eyes glittered with feral hunger, and his cheekbones were slashed with hot color. Every vestige of civilized male had been stripped away. He shuddered, closing his eyes as he imagined the moment when his body would penetrate hers.

She was so alive. He wanted some of that warmth for himself. Whether he had isolated himself deliberately or whether it had been a quirk of his birth order, he found it difficult to let people get close. With Cassidy, it was the opposite. He wouldn't be satisfied until they shared the same space, the same air, the same hushed anticipation.

His hair was still wet when he tucked a towel around his hips and returned to the living room. He found Cassidy sitting on the edge of a chair, feet planted flat on the floor, knees pressed together. She looked like a schoolgirl waiting for punishment to be doled out.

"Are you ready?"

She jerked when he spoke, as if she had been lost in thought. He saw her throat move as she swallowed. "Of course." She stood up so fast she stumbled and had to catch herself on the arm of the chair.

If he could have reached out a hand, he would have, but he was afraid that if he touched her, he would take her right there on the carpet. Extending an arm in the direction of the bedroom, he gave her what he hoped was a reassuring smile. "After you, Cass."

When she slid by him, careful not to touch, he caught a whiff of the shower gel he had rubbed over his own skin. The scent got in his head, imprinting her in his psyche.

Beside the king-size bed, she paused, her back to him. "Do you have condoms?"

"Of course." Though he had forgotten to fetch them from his shaving kit in the bathroom. In moments he rectified that glaring omission. Tossing a handful of packets onto the small bedside table, he glanced at the clock. It would be dawn soon.

Placing a hand on her narrow shoulder, he turned her around. Without her outrageous heels, the top of her head barely reached his collarbone. Using one finger, he tipped up her chin so he could see her eyes. Though she was by no means a helpless woman, her small frame seemed delicate next to his.

The expression in her gaze was difficult to read. Despite the fact that her hands rested trustingly at his waist, he sensed defensiveness in her posture. Perhaps she, too, saw the disparity in their physical sizes and felt threatened.

"I would cut off my arm before I would hurt you," he said. "I may be under the spell of a wicked arousal, but I'm not an animal. All you have to do is say *stop*…anytime. Do you believe me?"

She searched his face. "Yes," she said. Only that one word, but it was enough.

She had tied the sash of the robe tightly at her waist. If

the knot was supposed to slow him down, she didn't know much about men. He dispatched it in seconds and slid the entire garment off her shoulders and down her arms. When it fell to her feet, he thought he heard her gasp. Or maybe it was him.

All night he'd been desperate to hold her...to take her... to make her his. Now that the time had come, he had to pause a moment to take it all in. "You're beautiful," he said. The compliment was trite and commonplace and totally inadequate to convey the truth.

A more feminine woman, he had yet to find. Her skin was golden, a light, warm color that conjured up Italian olive groves and barefoot maidens running laughingly from ardor-filled suitors. Her glossy hair, black as a raven's wing, curled around his finger when he tested a strand.

He tried to fix his attention above her neck, but it was impossible not to notice the bounty below. Full, rounded breasts...curved hips...pert bottom. He scooped her into his arms, though the bed was no distance at all. It was a ploy to test the softness of her skin, to relish the naked magnificence that was Cassidy Corelli.

Her arms linked around his neck. "When do I get to undress *you*?"

"It's only a towel. I'm pretty sure we can manage."

"I notice it's kind of *poochy* in front."

Her mischievous teasing made him want to smile in the midst of his sexual frustration. "Are you calling me fat?" he asked, eyebrow raised.

"You don't seem to be in other places," she said. "But there's definitely a bulge beneath that terry cloth."

He flipped back the covers and dropped her on the bed. Her breasts jiggled nicely when she bounced. "Feel free to investigate."

Sprawling beside her, he settled on his back. What he

wanted was to pounce and take. But then again, anticipation was half of the pleasure. It took everything he had, even so, to feign relaxation.

Cassidy reared up on one elbow, fascination in her gaze as she looked him over. "I guess you work out." When she placed a hand, palm flat, on his abs, he flinched. It was too much and not enough.

"I'm not much for gyms," he said. "But where I live we spend a lot of time outdoors." His skin was several shades darker than hers for that reason. Except for a pale strip around his hips, he was tanned all over. He and his brothers had ranged free as kids, playing wild in the woods until they'd heard the bell summoning them to dinner.

She traced a scar below his rib cage. "What's this?"

"My brother Dylan shot me with a bow and arrow when we were in grade school."

"That's terrible," she exclaimed.

When she ran a fingertip over the puckered, long-ago-healed wound, he squirmed. "He didn't mean to. He was aiming for a squirrel. I ran into the line of fire at the wrong moment." The words were guttural, barely audible. He had broken out in a cold sweat, every cell in his body leaning toward the moment when she would remove the towel that tented lewdly upward.

Finally, when he thought he couldn't bear it a second longer, Cassidy curled her fingers beneath the edge of the damp towel and tugged. He lifted his hips. She finished the job.

"Holy crap." Her eyes widened. "Do you have a license to carry that thing?"

His penis was neither abnormally large nor embarrassingly small. But Cass stared at it as if she had unearthed a rare and exotic treasure. Her rapt regard increased its length and girth another increment.

"Trust me, Cassidy. We'll be a perfect fit."

Without replying, she wrapped one small hand around his shaft and squeezed lightly. He closed his eyes, holding his breath, as yellow spots danced against a black canvas. *God in heaven.* He was a goner.

Fluid leaked from the head. His would-be lover touched the slick wetness. Then she placed her fingertip in her mouth, tasting the evidence of his arousal. She seemed enthralled. Or perhaps postponing the inevitable out of some misguided notion that she was in control.

His patience eroded like sand in the midst of a storm. "Enough," he groaned. Forcing her onto her back, he used one hand to spread her thighs. Her sex was perfection, pink and wet and inviting. She smelled like lemons and need.

It never occurred to him to warn her before he tasted her essence. Her shriek might have awakened half the hotel had not the walls been so very well insulated. She shoved at his head. "Stop that. It tickles."

He had told her she could call a halt at any point. He just hadn't expected it to be now. Resting his forehead on her firm, soft thigh, he breathed harshly. "What's wrong? Surely you've had oral sex before."

"Of course I have. You startled me, that's all."

"Then may I continue?"

Her silence lasted about as long as it took earth to turn on its axis. Eons. Decades. "Cass?" He shivered like a man with ague.

"Yes…"

Her response was a tiny breathless syllable.

Returning to his task, he set about making her absolutely as insane as she had made him. Even as he pleasured her slowly, images filled his head. Driving hell-bent on a dark Nevada highway. Kissing wildly in the middle of the desert. Watching her body move like poetry in motion beneath that silver dress. Standing in front of an Elvis impersonator and promising forever.

At this precise moment all of it seemed perfectly reasonable.

He felt the instant when she neared the edge. Her hips lifted off the mattress. He held her down. Her breathing accelerated. He bit gently at the spot where she was most sensitive.

Holding Cassidy Corelli as she climaxed made every criticism he'd ever expressed about Vegas fade away into nothingness.

This was her town. And he'd staked a claim.

Four

Gavin shifted up in the bed so he could kiss her. On the mouth. The room was dim. When he moved his lips over hers, he was alarmed to taste salty tears. "Are you crying?" he asked, aghast.

She cupped his cheek. "Only a little," she whispered. "I didn't know it could feel that good."

"I haven't even gotten started yet." He said it to make her smile, but damned if it wasn't the truth.

"You're a dangerous man, Gavin Kavanagh."

"Dangerous how?"

"Addictive. Like gambling or alcohol."

"Are you saying I'm bad for you?"

"Maybe. Probably."

"Isn't that why people come to Vegas? To sow their wild oats? To cast off convention and morality? To take a walk on the wild side?"

As he argued his case, he stroked her breasts. They filled his hands as if she'd been created just for him. Not too large, not too small. He was beginning to think everything about her was eerily perfect. As if he were dreaming and any moment he would wake up and find the TV running some lower-than-B-movie porn flick.

He shook his head, trying to clear the fog and the feeling that he was letting down his guard at the worst possible moment. Cassidy's pert nipples fascinated him. Her little pants and groans urged him on as he played with the sensitive nubs.

She tossed her head, her hands gripping the sheets as he tormented them both. He usually preferred long hair on women, but Cass's chin-length curls framed her face and suited her personality so well, he couldn't imagine her any other way.

At last, he knew he couldn't hold out any longer. Testing her readiness with two fingers, he found her damp and welcoming. He grabbed a condom and rolled it on. As he moved between her legs and positioned himself at her entrance, he felt a flicker of unease. "Do you want this, Cass? No regrets in the cold light of day?"

At twenty-three, he'd been an immature ass. But Cassidy seemed far older than her years. Surely she knew her own mind.

Her smile was small but genuine. "I've never wanted anything more."

Surging forward, he cursed softly as the welcoming caress of her body squeezed him like a velvet fist. But icy shock slithered down his spine when he met with resistance. "Cassidy? Hell, Cass... Are you a...? Is this your...?"

Disbelief rendered him speechless. Along with another shot of suspicion and cynical doubt.

Slender legs wrapped around his waist. "Don't be mad. I know what I'm doing, Gavin. I realized not long after I set foot in your hotel room earlier tonight that I wanted you to be my first. It took me a little while to make up my mind, but I'm so glad I met you."

Something about that statement struck him at a raw spot, but he didn't have the mental acuity to process why. Instead, he focused on her deliberate omission. "Why didn't you tell me?"

"You would have left. Accused me of being too young for you. Done the noble thing and denied yourself."

To hear her assess him so accurately stung. "Or I would have taken what you offered regardless."

Her smile was wry. "I don't think so."

It wasn't as if he had a choice now. It would cripple him to leave this bed. Dazed and exhausted, he didn't have the strength of will to call a halt to things. She said she wanted this. And lord knows, he did.

Gently, he pressed forward. Her helpless wince stopped him cold. "I've never done this with a virgin," he croaked. "It's going to hurt you, Cass."

"Only for a minute. We'll muddle through, sweet man."

He was selfish and emotionally withdrawn and often cranky. Clearly, she didn't know him at all. He was torn in a dozen different directions. His body clawed for release like a junkie craving a hit. His brain shouted a warning. But Cass had done something to him. He couldn't bear the thought that this moment might be as bad for her as it was good for him.

Her fingernails dug into his butt cheeks. "It's okay, Gavin. I like it, really."

It was a brave lie, but nothing could disguise her cry when he pushed the final distance and found himself seated fully within her inner embrace. "I'm sorry, Cass," he muttered. It killed him to know he had caused her pain.

She wrinkled her nose. "It's not so bad now. I like how you feel inside me. Big and thick. Filling me up." Little flutters caressed his length as she exercised muscles that would give them both pleasure. "This is good. Truly. You've already given me an orgasm. It's your turn. Take what you need. I won't break."

Her altruism was charming but misguided. He would only go the distance if he could take her with him. He began to move slowly, shallow thrusts that applied pressure where her recent climax had left her ultrasensitive.

"Gavin!"

He knew the moment she crested again. Determined to make her forget the initial unpleasantness, he moved in her with care, staving off his own release until he felt her shudder and cry out.

Then it was all or nothing. He took her wildly, almost insensate, his world flaring into a hot white light before going black as incredible pleasure washed over him and carried him to a place of peace and unconsciousness.

Cassidy had done her share of impulsive things during her short life, but this was the most cataclysmic. Her body still hummed with aftershocks of sensation that made her toes curl against the soft cotton sheets.

Gavin Kavanagh was magnificent. Too bad she hadn't met him at a different time and place. If her father discovered that she had initiated sex with a virtual stranger, he would freak out, and he would certainly never take her seriously. He would question her judgment, and rightly so.

Now that school was done, it was the pivotal moment for her to take her long-coveted position at her father's side, despite her brother's wishes. It wasn't exactly a job that could be transferred cross-country, even if Gavin had been interested in more than a fling.

Still, she didn't have any regrets. Most of the guys she knew were shallow and egocentric. Boys, really. Not men. Not like Gavin. She ran a hand over his hard male chest, feeling the faint dusting of hair, the delineation of muscles, the flat belly. He was beautifully built.

When she moved lower to touch him more intimately, a large male hand clamped down on her wrist. "Give me five minutes, Cass. I haven't slept in over twenty-four hours and you just turned me inside out." But even as his rough-toned voice asked for mercy, his sex flexed and lifted.

"I wasn't rushing you," she said politely. "Just browsing the neighborhood." His bark of laughter made her smile. Somehow, she got the impression that Gavin Kavanagh was a pretty serious guy.

He started to lift up onto his elbows, but she pushed him back. "This one's on me," she said. The last thing she wanted was for him to see her as awkward or gauche. She tucked away her feelings of insecurity. Any woman worth her salt could pretend to be good in bed. Even if the major-ity of her knowledge was gleaned from books and movies.

Gavin rolled on a condom, and when he was ready, she climbed on top. Sliding down on him from this angle was very different. The brief discomfort was a small price to pay for the pleasure that was to come. She bounced experi-mentally. Gavin made a sound that was halfway between a curse and a prayer.

His fingers gripped her butt. "Why, Cass? Why me? Why now?" His jaw was firm, his expression suspicious and stubborn...as if he were prepared to chuck her out of his bed if he didn't like the answers.

What kind of man asked questions like that with a naked woman sitting on his chest?

She put her hands on his shoulders, kneading his flesh with giddy excitement. Already she could feel the be-ginning ripples of another orgasm. Some kind of serious pheromones were at work, because she wanted this beau-tiful man as she had never wanted anything in her life.

"I'll tell you, I swear," she said, panting. "But can we do this first? I think I'm having beginner's luck."

After that, any urge to talk disappeared. Gavin took charge. His arms were strong and his hips powerful. He held her and moved her and filled her with thrusts that built her hunger to a fever pitch. When she couldn't bear to wait another minute, he reached between them, touched her firmly at a certain spot, and then cradled her against his chest as they both came until there was nothing left.

She must have slept. At least for a few minutes. When she roused, Gavin was leaning over her with a washcloth, gently cleansing the residue of their lovemaking. His eyes were dark with concern as he saw the evidence of her innocence. Their eyes met…his shadowed, hers uncertain. It was a more profoundly intimate moment than any that had gone before.

When Gavin was satisfied that he had taken care of her, he tucked her up against his side, one big masculine arm holding her close. In moments his breathing became regular, but she couldn't tell if he was awake or asleep.

For the first time, misgivings winnowed their way to the surface, making her wince inwardly. What if this experience ruined her for other men? She couldn't imagine any other male of her acquaintance making her feel like this. Gavin was an intensely exciting lover. Both masterful and tender. At moments, it had been difficult to remember that she was her own person. All she had wanted was to lose herself in him.

The thought was sobering. She'd spent the past six years trying to prove her worth to her father. To make him see that a woman could be just as intelligent and business savvy as a man. But this gallant rescuer, her passionate lover, had shown her that in certain situations a woman might be tempted to chuck everything for the chance to be intimate with a man like Gavin.

She had planned out her career. She had goals and dreams. One day when her father was gone, Cassidy would be in charge of the casino. It was all she had ever wanted to do with her life.

But Gavin, damn him, made her question the master plan. Still, she shoved the doubts aside. She had gone into this experience with her eyes wide-open. This might not be casual sex on her part, but it was definitely temporary. It had to be. Her future didn't include a man who might try to mold her and change her and sidetrack her with his crazy hot body and phenomenal sex.

Her lover stirred and yawned, glancing at the illuminated dial of the clock beside the bed.

"What time is your flight?" she asked, feeling all her fuzzy happiness slip away.

"Eleven. Means I have to be there at ten."

"Not very long from now."

He linked his fingers with hers and lifted her hand to his lips. "Plenty of time for the big three."

"The big three?"

"I want to take you in the fancy tub, and the shower, and probably the sofa in the living room."

She actually felt faint. "Oh, well…"

He tugged one of her curls, tickling her ear with his fingertip. "But first, we talk."

"Talking is overrated. Though I do have a confession to make," she admitted, shamefaced.

He nuzzled her hair. "Then we'll start there."

It was difficult to know exactly what to say. "You know the man in the alley, the one you punched when you came to my rescue?"

"He's kind of hard to forget."

"That was my brother, Carlo."

The dead silence was intimidating. "Your brother was attacking you?" Gavin asked, the words enunciated carefully.

"Not exactly. We were arguing…loudly. Our family does that. I'm sure to an outsider it must have seemed as if I were in danger. So when you swooped in and rescued me, it was so sweet and wonderful and chivalrous."

"I hit an innocent man and left him on the ground. Yet you didn't bother to tell me the truth?" Gavin's volume escalated, his words incredulous. He rolled out of bed and got to his feet, pacing like a caged tiger. "Damn it, Cassidy. What were you thinking?"

The open accusation on his face brought hot tears to her eyes, but she blinked them back. "It all happened so fast," she said. "And trust me, Carlo is built like an ox. You didn't hurt him. When you dragged me back to your hotel room, I was enchanted. No man has ever stood up for me like that. I wanted to get to know you."

"You made a fool out of me," he said, his scowl black with displeasure.

"No. No, I didn't," she said, climbing off the mattress and going to him, trying to ignore her nudity and the shivery way it made her feel. She put both hands on his upper arms, wishing she had the strength to shake him out of his mood. "You acted on instinct. If the situation had been different, you would have saved me from something terrible."

Gavin thought himself far past being taken in by a pretty face. Yet here he was, suffering from the effects of bad judgment and simple lust. He'd been down this road before. A pretty girl, sexual attraction, a series of bad choices. As a senior at an Ivy League school in the Northeast, he'd spent time in jail when a woman accused him of rape.

The incident had nearly killed Gavin's mother. Even his own brothers had looked at him askance as if not quite sure what to make of the situation. The woman had been extremely convincing. Right up until the moment her lawyer promised to drop the charges against Gavin if the Kavanaghs handed over a hefty settlement.

Gavin had been furious and embarrassed and disgusted by the whole thing. He'd refused to let his family bail him out or pay anything to silence the duplicitous woman. For his stubbornness, he'd spent an unforgettable five nights behind bars. In hindsight, he should have tried harder to proclaim his innocence. The irony was, he'd never even had sex with the woman. They had dated only once.

Looking back, he could see that she had crossed his path intentionally, flirted with him and led him on. Her partner in crime, the alleged lawyer, was a fellow psychiatric patient with whom she had slipped away and, in a lucid moment, hatched a plan to get some money and disappear.

Fortunately for Gavin, the girl's parents had come forward when the story hit the newspapers. They lived in a nearby town where their daughter was institutionalized at a long-term care facility.

Gavin's pseudo girlfriend, faced with her parents' presence, finally recanted her story and Gavin was released. But the gossip had lived on. He hadn't dated much after that. Because every time he met a girl at school, there was always a look in her eyes…a question about Gavin's nature.

He'd responded to the situation by withdrawing into himself. He'd finished school and returned home to set up his cybersecurity business. He was good, very good. And once he was officially an adult, no one really cared about the unsavory incident in his past.

Yet, despite all he had learned, here he was again, standing on shaky ground. What if all that business at the wedding chapel had been some kind of setup? Was there an angry father or brother waiting just around the corner to insist on a shotgun wedding?

If was difficult to ignore the fact that a curvy beautiful

woman stood toe to toe with him, her breasts almost brushing his chest. "Put some clothes on," he said brusquely.

When he tried to turn away, Cassidy launched herself into his embrace, her arms locking around his neck. Though he was angry, his body responded predictably. Hunger roiled in his gut like an unappeased demon.

"Don't be like this," she cried. "We don't have much longer. Come back to bed."

Though he was stingingly aware of every inch of her voluptuous body plastered against his, he rallied his defenses, staring down at her with glacial disdain. Removing himself from her stranglehold, he stepped away. Cassidy's expression was chastened. As he watched, she grabbed a silk throw from the end of the bed and tucked it around her body like a sarong.

The ruby color made her skin glow.

Needing some armor himself, he picked up the damp towel from the floor and wrapped it around his hips as he had earlier. Grimacing at the clammy fabric, he crossed his arms over his chest. "I want to know," he said, keeping his tone level and unemotional, "how a woman who looks like you can still be a virgin at the age of twenty-three."

Cassidy perched on the end of the bed, one leg tucked beneath her. She was beautiful in an extremely natural and vibrant way. "It's simple, really. My dad is an extremely strict Italian Catholic father. My mother died when I was six. So Daddy sent me off to boarding school, followed by an all-girls college. It was only when I enrolled for my MBA that I had much contact with the opposite sex. And I was working so hard the whole two years that I didn't have much time for romance."

"So you remained pure as the driven snow." His sarcasm was a defense mechanism.

"I'm not saying I wasn't curious," Cass said. "But I

never really met anyone who tempted me enough to incur my father's wrath."

"What did you think he would do to you?"

"I didn't know. And I was scared to find out. I had body-guards assigned to me around the clock from the time I was first shipped away from Vegas. Daddy was afraid his status would make me an easy target for kidnappers. I rebelled, of course. But the one and only time I ever successfully eluded my guards and had a night out with girlfriends, my father came to campus and yelled at me for an hour, non-stop. That kind of thing leaves an impression."

"And after you graduated?"

"I wanted so badly to go into business with my father. I thought the MBA would convince him, but he has yet to promise me for sure that I'll have a spot at the casino."

"What about your brother?"

"Well, that's the infuriating part. I was a mama's girl, so when she died, I was lost. I was always *her* favorite and Carlo was Daddy's. Even though Carlo partied through school and majored in fraternity parties and binge drinking and women, he could do no wrong. I, on the other hand, worked my butt off. Carried a 4.0 all the way through. I wanted to prove to my father how ready I was to become his second in command."

"And did it work?"

"No. That's what Carlo and I were arguing about. He told me Daddy thinks I should marry and raise a family and leave the business end of things to Carlo."

"Maybe that's wishful thinking on your brother's part."

"I doubt it." Her expression was glum. "Daddy's very traditional. One of the floor managers is taking a two-week vacation starting next Friday. I'm hoping to cover for him while he's gone and prove that I can be an asset."

"So we've covered the reasons for your surprisingly virginal state, but not the specifics of *why me*? *Why now?*"

Five

Cassidy found that it was not an easy thing to carry on an adult conversation with a large, angry, half-naked man. She could understand his suspicions, but they were using up precious time.

She decided that honesty was the only prudent way to go. "I'm wildly attracted to you. From the first moment you ran down the street with me. You're gallant and wonderful and unlike any man I've ever met."

"And I'm leaving in the morning."

Grimacing, she nodded. "That played into it. No strings attached. When we got to your hotel room I realized that for once in my life I was going to take what I wanted and to hell with the consequences. I feel a connection with you, though I can't explain why. You're not much of a talker. But I knew that sex with you would be memorable."

Still he stared at her like judge and jury. "That's a pretty big step for the good little Catholic girl."

"I do want to prove myself to my father, but I'm a grown woman. My choices are mine." She paused, wondering if she had the guts to push this next point. "Admit it, Gavin. Tonight never would have happened if you hadn't been feeling some of the same things I was. You wanted me, too. That's what made it all so exciting."

The flicker of emotion in his eyes told her she had hit on the truth. The spark had come from both directions.

He glanced down at the place where the towel lifted over his erection. "It's a hard thing for a man to hide."

"I'd like to think I was more to you than a convenient body."

The silence stretched for miles. Just when she thought she would have to crawl into a hole to escape the humiliation, he nodded grudgingly. "You're a fascinating woman, Cass. Intensely feminine, distractingly sexual. But from where I'm standing, this all seems a little too good to be true. I can't help wondering if there's a trap in here somewhere."

She stood up, hoping his compliments meant an end to hostilities. "I swear on my mother's grave that I am no threat to you at all. And I've told you the whole truth and nothing but the truth. Do you believe me?"

He ran his gaze from her head to her toes, making everything in between sizzle with excitement. Her skin hummed with the need to feel him inside her again.

"I want to believe you. Though I have damn little reason to do so. But even if you turn out to be my worst mistake, I can't walk away now. Your promises will have to do." When he ripped off the towel a second time, she should have been prepared. But his body was a sculptor's dream.

She swallowed hard. "I'm glad."

With his hands on his hips, he studied her. Then, before she had a chance to prepare, he closed the distance between them in two long strides and plucked away her only armor, leaving her defenseless and bare in more ways than one.

He scooped her into his arms. "The hot tub will help you feel better." He kissed her briefly, a butterfly brush of lips to lips.

His breath was warm on her cheek. She looked up into

his eyes searching for something…anything. Was he sorry to be leaving?

In the bathroom, he turned on the taps. The oversize faucet dispensed water generously. While they waited for the tub to fill, Gavin perched on the edge and stood her between his legs. With his hands on her waist, he proceeded to rekindle her need.

Rough tongue on sensitive nipples. Murmured words of praise and admiration. His thumbs rubbed her hip bones in a desultory fashion as if there was all the time in the world for foreplay.

She rested her forehead against his. For the first time, she realized with no small amount of dismay that grabbing for what she wanted had a downside. "The sand in the hourglass is almost gone," she whispered. "I'll never forget this night."

His body went rigid, his rapid shallow breaths audible. "Pretend we have forever, Cass." He buried his face between her breasts. "That's all you have to do."

Gavin put a hand to his head and groaned. The muted chirping of the alarm on his cell phone had awakened him. Studying the screen, bleary-eyed, he saw that he barely had enough time to shower and shave and head to the airport to turn in his rental car.

He rolled toward Cass, determined to take her one more time despite the time crunch. Last night had been amazing, perhaps the best of his life.

But when he reached across the bed, he found nothing but empty, chilled sheets. Abruptly, the sleep fog lifted. "Cass," he called out urgently, hoping she was in the bathroom.

Then he saw the note on her pillow. His stomach pitched

unpleasantly. The small rectangle of hotel notepaper had been folded once. He opened it and read:

Dear Gavin:
Last night was amazing. I've never met a man like you. I'm sorry for not being totally honest with you in the beginning…about everything…but I selfishly wanted a chance to spend time with you. I suppose you think badly of me, but I hope in time you'll be able to forgive me and to enjoy the memories of our one incredible night in Vegas.

I know you have a plane to catch, so I didn't linger. I never have liked goodbyes anyway. I hope the women in North Carolina appreciate you as much as I do. You are one in a million.
Fondly,
Cassidy Corelli

He dropped the Dear John letter on the bed and put his head in his hands. This was the kind of experience many men craved—the gorgeous woman, the no-strings sex, the night of unparalleled excess. He should be feeling on top of the world.

But the truth was, this trip to Vegas sucked, any way you looked at it. Stumbling into the bathroom, he splashed water on his face and then stared in the mirror as he grabbed a hand towel. He looked like hell. Bloodshot eyes underscored by dark circles. Stubbly chin. A headful of hair sticking up in all directions.

If he'd just scored #1 on the all-time list of guy fantasies, then why did he feel like crap? And why was his gut telling him he'd made a gargantuan mistake?

He slept his way across the country. Flying first class at least gave him room to stretch out his legs and get semi-comfortable. The young blonde flight attendant flirted with him. He passed up the offers for alcohol and peanuts and instead propped his head against the window.

Changing planes in Atlanta was a hassle, but at least no one paid any attention to him. He bought the latest hardcover crime thriller so he could use it as a shield if necessary.

Once he landed in Asheville, he sent a text to his brother Conor, who was picking him up. In Conor's hybrid SUV on the way to Silver Glen, all Gavin wanted to do was brood. But Conor was cheerful and chatty and interested in hearing about the trip.

Gavin answered in single syllables, hoping his sibling would take the hint, but it was not to be.

Finally, Conor shot him a frowning glance and called him on his crappy attitude. "What the hell's wrong with you, Gavin?"

"Sorry," he muttered, suddenly ashamed of his mood. "I guess I'm just tired."

"Don't try that on me. Something is chewing your ass and I want to know what it is. Did your speech crash and burn?"

"No. Everyone loved it."

"Don't tell me you gambled and lost a pile of money. That doesn't sound like you at all."

Gavin managed a grin. "I never even put a nickel in a slot machine. If I want to blow money, I'll toss it out the window on the interstate."

"Then what?" Conor demanded, changing lanes to avoid a semitruck going twenty miles under the speed limit.

"Did it ever occur to you that it might be personal?"

Conor whistled as his eyebrows shot up to his hairline. "Good lord. It's a woman, isn't it?"

Not just any woman, but a sparkling, funny, utterly de-

lightful female who made him second-guess everything he knew about himself.

"Of course not," Gavin lied. "It was being in Vegas. Everything artificial and garish and frantic. I didn't want to go in the first place, and I'm damn glad to be home. Give me a good night's sleep, and I'll be back to normal in the morning."

Conor frowned, but kept his eyes on the road. "Fine. Don't tell me. But you'd better be more convincing when you talk to Mom, because she can sniff out a lie better than a bloodhound."

Cassidy covered her mouth with one hand, swallowing hard to keep from throwing up. She sat on the end of a vinyl-covered exam table, her modesty protected only by a thin paper gown.

"Could you please say that again?" she whispered.

Dr. Landau, the man who had been her pediatrician since birth, gave her a look laced with considerable concern. "You're pregnant, Cassidy. Didn't you suspect?"

"No, sir. Daddy is finally letting me take on more responsibility at the casino, and I've been working crazy hours. I just assumed it was stress. I'm not all that regular anyway."

The gray-haired, kindly physician had been telling her since she turned eighteen that she needed to find a general practitioner and an ob-gyn, but Cassidy loved Dr. Landau. Where her father bellowed and blustered, Dr. Landau was invariably gentle and professional.

He shook his head, his expression wry. "I'm retiring at the end of the year, Cassidy. I appreciate the fact that you and I have known each other for two decades, but you're a grown woman and you must find appropriate medical care. You have another person to think about now."

"How far along am I?" She knew the answer down to a five-hour period, but she wanted to hear it from him.

"About ten weeks, I think. You'll want to get an ultrasound soon. I can prescribe prenatal vitamins, but I need you to promise me that you'll call and set up an appointment with an obstetrician. Soon."

"I will, I swear. I thought I had a stomach virus. I never dreamed…" She trailed off, feeling foolish and alone and frightened.

Dr. Landau frowned. "How long have you been sexually active, Cassidy?"

She shrugged, her face heating. "Just about ten weeks."

He shook his head. "Isn't that the way it works? Couples try for years to get pregnant and others who aren't even thinking in that vein wind up with a surprise on the way. You have options, of course. But you'll want to discuss those with the father."

"He's not really in the picture."

The doctor didn't seem particularly judgmental, but Cassidy felt guilty anyway. She'd spent her entire life playing by the rules, and one impulsive night had brought her to this.

Dr. Landau stood. "Go ahead and get dressed. I'll have my nurse bring in the vitamin prescription." He paused. "You know I can't discuss anything we've said here with your father. But he's my friend. And you're going to need support no matter which way you decide to go. To be honest, you shouldn't spend another hour working in the casino. Secondhand smoke can be harmful to your baby."

"I understand," Cassidy said as panic clawed at her throat. "Thank you for seeing me today." An era of her life was ending. Though she had considered herself focused and mature and ready to assume the full mantle of adulthood, clearly there were aspects she hadn't considered.

When the doctor exited the exam room, she put on her clothes and glanced in the mirror on the back of the door. She didn't *look* pregnant. She didn't *feel* pregnant. She was, however, miserably sick and confused and desperate. What was she going to do?

As she drove home to the elaborate house she shared with her father and brother, her brain ran in circles. She was supposed to stand by her father's side, preparing to run the business in his retirement. She had trained for that, worked hard for that.

A baby had never figured into the plan. In fact, she had assumed she wouldn't have children. She knew her father's traditional values wouldn't allow him to choose her as his successor if she had a family. He'd think she needed to be with her children. So she had focused on working toward her father's legacy.

Keeping one hand on the steering wheel, she placed the other flat on her stomach. A new life. A baby. No matter the upheaval in her world, she would never consider terminating the pregnancy. She couldn't. Clearly Gavin had no interest in a relationship with her since there had been no contact between him and Cassidy since he left.

So only two choices remained…becoming a single mother, or giving the infant up for adoption. Even as she pondered it, a wave of maternal instinct washed over her, bonding her for the first time with the tiny boy or girl growing in her womb.

This child was *hers*. Hers and Gavin's, to be correct. The only thing she knew for certain was that she would keep the child. She would have to tell him. Eventually. But not until she had time to get her act together.

After dinner prepared by the housekeeper and served in the formal dining room, Cassidy and her father and Carlo adjourned to the family room. It was an unabashedly masculine enclave, but in one corner sat the Disney toy box that had housed Cassidy's dolls and such as she grew up.

Carlo was busy on his cell phone. Gianni Corelli lit a cigar and sat back in his overstuffed leather recliner. The smell of the Havana tobacco sent Cassidy dashing for the nearest bathroom to lose the contents of her stomach. When she returned, she was shaking, but moderately in control.

Neither male paid her much attention. They saw each other at work on and off all day. The evenings were for winding down, though often one or all of them would return to the casino toward midnight to see how things were going.

She wanted to ask Carlo to leave. It was going to be hard enough to break the news to one person, much less two. Her father's reaction was going to be ugly. But she couldn't think of any plausible reason to ask for privacy.

Finally, when tension knotted her belly and anxiety dampened her forehead, she blurted it out. "Daddy... Carlo...I have something to tell you." It took a few seconds, but both men looked up and focused their attention on her face.

Her father smiled genially. "What is it, *mia bella figlia*? I have had many compliments on your job performance the last two months. I suppose all that fancy education I paid for was worth it."

Carlo scowled. "I work, too."

His father gave him a grin. "Of course you do. Mostly coaxing young pretty tourists to try their luck at the roulette wheel. We all have our strengths, son."

Cassidy could tell that her father's patronizing tone irked Carlo, but her brother held his tongue. Luckily for him, in a few moments he was going to be out of the line of fire.

"Thank you, Daddy. I'm glad you're pleased."

"So," he said, tapping his cigar in an ashtray. "You have my attention."

There was really no way to ease into this. She swallowed, feeling nausea swirl in her tummy again. "I'm pregnant."

In hindsight, perhaps a letter might have been the better choice. Her father's florid complexion turned an alarming shade of puce. "I will kill the boy," he said, his dark eyes flashing fire. "Who is he? Who dared defile my baby girl?"

Cassidy wanted to roll her eyes, but she restrained the impulse. Why was this household always filled with drama? "I'm not defiled, Daddy. I'm pregnant. There's a difference. And he's not a boy. He's a man. I made a mistake and now I have to accept the consequences. But I want this baby. I really do."

Carlo had been struck dumb, perhaps alarmed by his father's apoplectic rage. For once, Cassidy's competitive brother didn't speak up. Maybe because he could already see the benefits for himself in this situation.

Gianni Corelli got to his feet, his hands clenched in fists. "You will correct this situation," he hissed.

Cassidy backed up a step. "I don't know what you mean." It broke her heart to see the man who had raised her stare with such open antagonism.

"You will go to him," he said. "Find the bastard and tell him what he has done to you. And you will not set foot in this house again until you are either engaged or married."

"But, Daddy…"

He held up a hand, his body quaking with fury. "Your dear mother, God rest her soul, would turn over in her grave if she could see you now. You have shamed our home."

At last, Carlo spoke, surprisingly in defense of his sister. "Take it easy, Papa. This isn't the Middle Ages. You're going to have a stroke if you don't calm down."

Unfortunately for Cassidy, much as she appreciated her brother's support, it didn't help the situation.

Her father held out an arm, pointing at the door. "Go. Pack a bag. Be gone by morning. I will cancel your credit cards. You may use the money in your personal account."

Cassidy gaped. That would be less than two thousand dollars. Her father hadn't wanted her to work while she was in school. He'd insisted that she concentrate on her studies. "But I—"

"This isn't up for discussion, daughter. You will make this right or you will never again be welcome under this roof."

Cassidy began to cry. Never in a million years had she expected this reaction. She knew her father was old-school and traditional and strict. He had been twenty years older than her mother when they married, and he was very much set in his ways. But he loved his daughter…didn't he?

Carlo took her arm, steering her out of harm's way when she was too stunned to walk on her own. His bedroom was first down the hallway. He urged her inside and shut the door. "If you'll tell me where you need to go, I'll put a plane ticket on my credit card." He opened a bureau drawer and withdrew a wad of cash. "This should help. And you can call me if you need more."

Cassidy sniffed, her emotions all over the map. "Why are you being so nice to me?"

Carlo gave her a lopsided grin. "You're my sister. Father has pitted us against each other our whole lives, but those things he said to you in there are wrong. I love you, Cass. You'll get through this. Don't worry."

It was a strange and wonderful sensation to feel her brother's arms around her as she sobbed. She felt a little less alone. A little less desperate. At last, she pulled back and wiped her eyes. "Thank you."

"Where shall I book a ticket to?"

"Asheville, North Carolina." She had already studied a map when she had been moping over losing Gavin. Asheville was the largest town of any size near Silver Glen.

"One-way, or with an open-ended return?"

"One-way, I suppose. I have no idea how this is going to turn out. I can't just tell this guy he has to marry me."

Carlo tugged her hair as he had when they were kids. "You'll find a solution. You always do. And besides, your baby daddy may be glad to see you. Who knows?"

Six

Gavin swung the ax with all his might, feeling the reverberation in his shoulders as the sharp blade cleaved the oak log. Beside him lay a three-foot-high stack of firewood that would season over the spring and summer and be ready for his fireplace come fall.

Sweat poured down his back both from exertion and from the heat of the sun in a cloudless sky. No matter how hard he pushed himself, he couldn't escape the memories that tormented him. His luxurious house high on the mountainside was usually a refuge. Since returning from Nevada, though, it had become a prison.

Even his demanding work, normally a stimulating and distracting challenge, failed to keep him from thinking about *her*. Young, sassy, exuberant Cassidy Corelli. She had bewitched him. There was no other explanation. And though he knew for a fact that a man couldn't become a husband without a license and other legal considerations, he couldn't erase the memory of standing in front of an altar and promising to love, honor and cherish. It had been a silly, dangerous game.

The ax glanced off a knot in the wood, narrowly escaping the toe of his boot. This was not a good time to lose focus.

A half hour later, he called a halt. After a shower and

a sandwich, he was prepared to hole up in his office and work until he was tired enough to sleep without dreaming.

He was in the kitchen smearing peanut butter over a slice of wheat bread when the doorbell rang. Frowning, he wiped his hands on a dish towel and headed for the front of the house. His hair was still damp, and he wasn't wearing a shirt, but it was probably a delivery person of some sort.

When he swung wide the door, his hand clenched the edge of the frame until his knuckles turned white. "Cassidy. What are you doing here? How did you find me?"

She looked like hell, to be honest. Her skin had lost its glow and her beautiful eyes were dull with fatigue. Even the sheen of her wavy dark hair was dulled. At her feet sat a small rolling suitcase. The simple navy knit dress she wore was sleeveless in deference to the weather. Over one arm she carried a khaki raincoat.

"May I come in?" she asked.

The words were polite and proper. Not in the least intimating that the two of them had once upon a time been naked together. He wanted to grab her up and smother her adorable bow-shaped lips with wild kisses, but his innately suspicious nature kicked in.

"Of course," he said, stepping back.

Cassidy's gaze landed on his chest and danced away. She was careful not to touch him as she slipped past him into the formal living room. "Thank you."

He indicated a chair. "Have a seat."

It was disconcerting as hell to realize that he was hard already. Just from looking at her. Hopefully the heavy denim would disguise his ill-timed response. He didn't know why she had come, but judging by her expression, it wasn't to have another round of crazy, impetuous sex.

She put down her purse and bag and sat in silence, her gaze cataloging the contents of the room. He tried not to notice the way a single curl tickled her chin. "Is this a social visit?"

At last, she looked at him. Her teeth sank into her lower lip. Small graceful hands twined in her lap. "Not exactly."

"How are things going at the casino? With your father... and your job?"

"Great. Or they were." Now she appeared stricken.

Rubbing a hand across the back of his neck, he sighed. "I don't mean to be rude, but you're confusing the hell out of me. I thought we were ships that passed in the night. You made it very clear that you were focused on your work and on getting ahead of your brother. You never gave me any indication that you wanted to see me again."

Tears welled in her beautiful eyes. "I'm pregnant, Gavin."

She saw him turn white. Any burgeoning hope that he might be glad to see her shriveled and died. "Say something," she said.

"Are you telling me you think I'm the father?"

Her stomach turned to stone. "Of *course* that's what I'm saying. You were there, Gavin. You know I was innocent."

The skepticism in his frigid stare cut deep. "That was weeks ago. Doesn't mean there hasn't been someone else in the meantime." He paused, his expression going from disapproval to grim suspicion. "Have you forgotten that we used protection every time?"

She sat there stunned, gaping at him. The man who had made love to her in a Las Vegas hotel room with such tender passion had nothing in common with this hard-eyed stranger. She'd naively thought he might be glad to see her. Her throat was so tight she couldn't speak for several long seconds. But she lifted her chin and met his gaze bravely. "Except for that time in the hot tub. Remember?"

From the flicker in his eyes, she could see that he did. But the memory did nothing to soften his stance. Despite the fact that he had been sexy and funny and wonderful and irresistible when he had claimed her beneath the swirling water that night, he was anything but at the moment.

When he said nothing, she held out her hands. "Why would I lie about this?"

"Maybe you found out that the Kavanaghs are wealthy. Maybe you wanted a free ride."

"My father has enough money to buy and sell Silver Glen several times over."

"Then why are you here?"

His stony gaze made her angry. "I thought you might want to know that you were going to be a father. It seemed like important information. But if you don't give a damn, I've wasted a trip."

She leaped to her feet, feeling like a naive idiot. The knight in shining armor who had rescued her in a Vegas alley had nothing in common with this antagonistic man.

Before she could reach the door, he blocked her exit, inserting his big, intimidating self between her and the escape route. "Wait."

One word. Flat. Unemotional.

She pulled up short. "I know this isn't something you wanted, Gavin. If I'm being brutally honest, I didn't want it, either. But I'm pregnant, and I'm not going to make an innocent child pay for my mistakes."

Something about the line of his jaw softened. "Is that what I was to you? A mistake?"

"What would you call it?"

He rubbed a hand across his chin, for the first time betraying a hint of rueful self-derision. "Momentary insanity?"

They stared at each other, the past vivid and alive. In

his eyes she saw the truth of what he wasn't saying. He remembered all too well. Just as she did. The laughter and intimate touches they had shared. Hushed groans. Wild cries of pleasure. Sated, drowsy satisfaction in the aftermath.

Now that he had momentarily dropped his guard, he looked far more approachable. He folded his arms across his chest. "I'm sorry if I've been less than welcoming. I want you to stay for a while. If you're telling the truth, we'll have things to discuss. Plans to make."

Despite the *if* in his response, his about-face in terms of hospitality sent relief washing over her. The nausea she'd been fighting for days resurfaced. "Bathroom," she said hoarsely, her hand clamped over her mouth.

He read the situation instantly. Pointing to a door across the foyer, he followed on her heels as she made a dash for the facilities. Emptying her stomach for the third time that day left her wrung out and exhausted.

Gavin helped her to her feet, handed her a damp washcloth and steered her to the kitchen, where he gently pushed her into a chair and poured her a glass of cold water. Through it all, he didn't say a word. But his quiet empathy took the edge off her embarrassment.

"Thank you," she muttered.

He propped a hip against the counter. "Has it been bad?"

"You could say that."

"You've lost weight."

The man had seen her naked. His dispassionate comment shouldn't have made her blush, but it did. "I could stand to lose a few pounds."

Gavin shook his head. "Not that I recall."

Suddenly, the world shifted and they were back in the desert on a dark night, racing along the highway. She experienced the same sense of anticipation, the same feeling of wonder.

When it seemed as if her stomach was going to cooperate, she grimaced. "I want to be honest with you about everything. My father has kicked me out of the house. Carlo took my place at the casino. Apparently I've besmirched the Corelli family name. I think I was supposed to walk out into the desert and die for my sins, but I've never been the self-sacrificing type."

Gavin still reeled from Cassidy's revelation, but growing up with six brothers, he had learned to keep a poker face. Never had that ability stood him in better stead than now.

He'd spent only one night with her, but even he knew how important it was for her to win her father's approval. It was hard to imagine the hurt she had suffered and the feelings of being adrift with this latest development.

And then there was his own bizarrely blank reaction. He was going to be a father. No matter how many times he said the words in his head, they didn't seem real. His brother Liam had a kid. And Dylan had adopted his bride's little girl. Aidan and Emma were expecting. But that didn't make it Gavin's turn. Not at all.

He wasn't cut out for parenthood.

Looking at Cassidy made him ache. Even dimmed, her beauty and spirit tugged at his heartstrings. If anything, the touch of vulnerability in her weary posture added another layer to her appeal.

"You can stay as long as you need to," he said quietly, wondering if he was condemning himself to weeks of sexual frustration. He'd acted out of character once in his life, creating an enormous mess. No point in compounding the mistake.

"I'm sure my father will relent eventually. For once, Carlo is on my side. He'll plead my case."

"What exactly does Mr. Corelli want from you?"

Cass's cute turned-up nose wrinkled. "He told me not to come home until I was engaged or married."

Gavin froze, his heart pounding in his chest. "You're joking, right?"

"I wish I were. My father is very old-school traditional."

For a moment, Gavin wondered if Cassidy was going to bring up their visit to the wedding chapel. Again, he reminded himself he couldn't believe everything she said. What if this whole thing was a scam? A setup?

"I don't know you, Cassidy," he said flatly. "And you don't know me. I hope you'll understand when I say we need to get a paternity test.

Though she winced, she nodded. "It's not necessary, but if it will make you feel better..."

"Can we do it while you're pregnant?"

"It's possible, I think. One tests the placenta and the other the amniotic fluid. But both procedures carry a small risk of miscarriage."

"Then we'll wait."

"For months?"

"Do you have a better solution?"

She sagged into the chair. "I suppose not. But what am I supposed to do in the meantime?"

"I don't know. What do other pregnant women do? Read books? Design nursery plans?"

Her eyes flashed. "I worked my butt off for six straight years of college. Is that degree useless now? Just because you and I did something stupid?"

He sympathized with her plight. He really did. But no matter the equality of the sexes, a woman always had to bear a greater share of the burden when it came to children. Especially if she planned on nursing the baby.

Imagining Cassidy with an infant at her breast was not

a good idea. When he realized his hands were shaking, he shoved them in his pockets. "Your degree will keep. In the meantime, you can explore Silver Glen. We'll need to find you a doctor very soon. Have you had an ultrasound yet?"

"No. I'd like you to be with me for that." She looked at him with such naked hope, that he wanted to reassure her. This moment should be joyful. And it would be so easy to let her back into his life. Her presence in his house would ensure warmth and light.

Though he couldn't say it out loud, he reluctantly admitted to himself that he had missed her. He wanted badly to believe her...to accept that he was her baby's father. But he'd been naive about a woman's sincerity once before and had paid dearly for his mistake.

"I'll be happy to go with you," he said. There was tenderness in his voice despite his reservations. No matter how hard he had tried not to, he remembered every second of the time she had spent in his bed. And how she had made him feel. He hadn't allowed himself to acknowledge how special it was, because there had been no choice but to let her go. Now she was here, and he could no longer pretend that the night in Vegas was ordinary. If the baby *was* his, life was about to get very complicated.

"I'm tired." Cassidy's emotions were written on her face. Despair. Disappointment. Had she expected him to welcome her with open arms? Not even a sheltered twenty-three-year-old could be that optimistic.

"I'll show you to a guest suite. You'll have plenty of privacy. The room has its own bath." His house wasn't all that large. But he'd built it sparing no expense when it came to comfort and luxury. Top-of-the-line everything. At least he could offer Cassidy the safety and security of a pleasant place to lay her head.

He knew his reserve hurt her. Maybe she really was exactly what she seemed. Gavin had been her first lover. No doubt about that. But she might have moved on quickly. She was a sensual woman, and he had awakened her sexual nature. It wouldn't be unusual if she'd exercised her new-found knowledge with a longtime boyfriend.

He still couldn't explain why she'd chosen Gavin and that particular Vegas night to change her status, but he liked to think it was because she saw something in him that she wanted…that she needed.

The two of them together had been incendiary. Sexual chemistry off the charts. But that didn't mean she had been celibate in the meantime.

What did it say about him that he hoped desperately he was wrong? If he let her know how much he wanted to believe her story, he'd be handing over power he wasn't ready to cede. Better to advance cautiously and see what happened.

"If you're feeling steadier now," he said, "I'll help you get settled." He ushered her down the hall and opened a door. "Will this do?"

The room was neither masculine nor feminine. But its muted shades of lemon and eggshell blue exuded a sense of serenity. He'd had help with the decor, and he was pleased with how it had turned out.

Cassidy scanned the furnishings with a small smile. "It's lovely," she said.

"I'll fetch your bags."

When he returned to the guest room, he found Cassidy bent over, one hand on the bed, slipping out of her shoes. It was a maneuver he had come to expect from her. She didn't see him at first, so he studied her freely. Though she was competent and smart, he sensed that her impending motherhood was weighing on her.

What did a man know about such things? He would

never understand what it meant to carry a baby for nine months. To feed the little boy or girl. To form a bond long before the day of birth arrived.

As a quintessential middle child, he'd forged his own way in life. Though he loved his family, he'd never felt as connected as he ought to be. Would it be any different if he had a son or daughter? His own father had been selfishly obsessed with chasing dreams of long-lost silver mines. The pursuit had cost him his life.

Gavin lived alone and liked it. He worked all hours of the day and night, answering to no one, except maybe his mother, Maeve, who was constantly trying to keep him involved in family events and telling him he spent too much time as a hermit. Lord knows what she would think about Gavin's houseguest.

Having Cassidy beneath his roof would play havoc with his life. He'd be tormented by images of her just down the hall. Sleeping in a bed he'd provided, getting naked in a shower he'd designed.

Holy hell. He was doomed.

She must have heard him, because she straightened suddenly and faced him, barefoot and beautiful. "I thought I'd take a nap," she said. "If you don't mind."

"Of course not. My office is at the back of the house. Let me know if you need anything."

She didn't blink an eye at his unwittingly suggestive offer. "I will."

Seven

Cassidy didn't realize she was holding her breath until the door closed behind Gavin. She sank into a blue-and-white toile-covered armchair and put her hands over her face. *Well, that went well.*

Surely there was no greater humiliation than puking in the presence of the man to whom she'd just given not-so-welcome news. Gavin had been in turns stoic and quietly compassionate.

But what he *hadn't* been was happy to see her. Perhaps she hadn't admitted to herself how much she was hoping for a fairy-tale ending. Which made no sense at all, because she and Gavin had spent less than twenty-four hours together. He was right. They didn't know each other.

In his shoes, she would have demanded a paternity test, as well.

Even so, the day had lost its fizz. Despite the upheaval in her life, she had been excited about traveling to Silver Glen and giddy about the prospect of seeing Gavin again. But it was painfully clear that their brief encounter in Vegas had meant nothing to him other than physical release.

She certainly hadn't spent the intervening weeks doodling her initials and his on napkins. Responsibilities at the casino had kept her busy for a succession of fourteen-hour days. She'd thrown herself into the family business with gusto, convinced that her father recognized her worth as an employee and an equal. But amid all that, it had been impossible to forget meeting Gavin.

Images from the night they spent together popped into her head at random moments, making her cheeks heat and her core tighten. He was not an easy man to forget.

Now, stripping down to her underwear, she climbed under the covers and tried to rest. One of the biggest problems with her pregnancy so far—in addition to the nausea—was an all-encompassing fatigue. That was partly the reason she hadn't thought twice about the fact that she had missed a period. She'd been stressed and exhausted, but determined not to show it.

Today, however, she had slept on the plane. Because of that, she only dozed lightly now, her mind darting from one subject to the next. Where would she live? Would her father relent? How much, if any, of a role would Gavin want to play in his child's life?

She was normally an optimistic person, but it was hard to see a way out of this. She had never anticipated being a single mom. In fact, she had never planned on being a mom at all. Though several of her friends were eager to start families, Cassidy's main goal in life had been to become her father's right-hand man. Or in this case, woman.

But that was part of the problem. Though her father loved her, she knew he didn't really think a female should shoulder serious responsibilities in the workforce if she was of childbearing age. Italians loved children. And they revered Madonna figures. In Mr. Corelli's estimation, there was no higher calling than to be called *Mother*.

Well, Cassidy couldn't argue about the importance of that role. But she wanted more. Was that such a crime? Growing up without a mother had made her painfully aware of how important it was for a girl to have a female parent. Since Cassidy was a realist, she deduced that she couldn't pursue her goal of one day running the casino and being a mom at the same time, because of her father's old-fashioned values.

So she made a choice. She chose career over home and hearth.

But what happened now?

At last, when it became clear that she wasn't really sleepy, she climbed out of bed and rummaged in her suitcase for gray yoga pants and a hip-length solid T-shirt in bright teal. Though some of her clothes were only now beginning to feel a little tight, the ever-present nausea meant that a loose-fitting wardrobe offered a degree of comfort.

Barefoot, she tiptoed down the hall toward the rear of the house. It wasn't difficult to locate Gavin. The door to his office stood open. She paused in the doorway and gawked.

On the far wall, a bank of no less than a dozen television screens were mounted in three rows. One of them played a popular news program. A second was linked to the Weather Channel. The other ten or so displayed what looked to Cassidy like gibberish. Gavin was focused on his work.

Surrounded by laptops and desktops and stacks of paper, he appeared to be multitasking without breaking a sweat. Knocking lightly at the door so as not to startle him, she crossed the threshold.

He swirled to face her. "Cassidy. Sorry, I didn't hear you."

"You were deep in thought. Am I interrupting?"

He shrugged. "Not particularly." He waved a hand at the leather executive chair that matched his. "Sit down. Did you nap?"

"A little." The bland conversation was polite and frustrating. Gavin looked masculine and gorgeous in jeans and a cotton sweater in a pale shade of green.

He ran his hands through his hair, rumpling it and making him look even sexier…as if he had recently rolled out of bed. "I forgot to mention that the kitchen is pretty well-stocked," he said. "You should help yourself to anything that sounds good to you."

"Do you cook?"

"Only when necessary. I have a weekly housekeeper who leaves things in my freezer that I can heat up. Sometimes I go eat at the Silver Beeches Lodge. And if I'm in the mood for pub food, my brother Dylan owns the Silver Dollar Saloon. I don't starve."

"I could fix some meals while I'm here. It would make me feel like I'm earning my keep."

"It's not necessary. But please feel free to do anything that entertains you."

"I'm not a child," she snapped, his last comment catching her on the raw. "I don't have to be distracted with pony rides and ice cream."

Her temper elicited a grin from her oh-so-serious host. "I don't own any livestock, and I'm lactose intolerant."

"Don't patronize me."

The madder she got, the more genuine his smile. It infuriated her.

"You know why we're squabbling, don't you?" he asked, cocking his head and staring at her with a gaze hot enough to make her squirm in her chair.

"Because you're an ass?"

"Ouch." He shook his head. "I brought you in and offered you food and lodging. And this is the thanks I get?"

She took a deep breath. "I'm sorry," she said formally. "I've disturbed your work. I'll go back to my room."

Without warning, Gavin stood up. Suddenly the office shrank in size. His personality and masculine presence sucked up all the available oxygen. Pacing so near her chair that he almost brushed her knees, he muttered beneath his breath.

"What did you say?" Probably something uncomplimentary about his unexpected houseguest.

He shot her a look laden with frustration. "We need some ground rules, Cassidy. First of all, we're going to forget that we've ever seen each other naked."

She gulped, fixating on the dusting of hair where the shallow V neckline of his sweater revealed a peek of his chest. "I'm pretty sure that's going to be the elephant in the room. Our night in Vegas was amazing. Maybe not for you, but for me. Telling me to forget it is next to impossible."

"Good lord, woman. Don't you have any social armor at all?"

"I am not a liar. If you want me to pretend we haven't been intimate, I'll try, but I make no promises."

He leaned over her, resting his hands on the arms of the chair. His beautifully sculpted lips were in kissing distance. Smoke-colored irises filled with turbulent emotions locked on hers like lasers. "I may be attracted to you, Cass, but I don't completely trust you. It's too soon. So, despite evidence to the contrary, I do have some self-control."

Maybe *he* did, but hers was melting like snow in the hot sun. His coffee-scented breath brushed her cheek. This close, she could see tiny crinkles at the corners of his eyes. She might have called them laugh lines if she could imagine her onetime lover being lighthearted enough and smiling long enough to create them.

"You're crowding my personal space," she said primly.

For several seconds, she was sure he was going to steal a kiss. Her breathing went shallow, her nipples tightened and a tumultuous feeling rose in her chest. Not nausea.

Something far more volatile. For the first time, she understood that whatever madness had taken hold of them in Las Vegas was neither a fluke nor a onetime event.

Gavin still wanted her. As much as she wanted him. But he wasn't happy about it.

At long last, he moved away. "I'm sorry."

She was sorry, too. Sorry he hadn't dragged her to the carpet and had his wicked way with her. Pregnancy hormones could be a blessing and a curse. Right now she wanted Gavin with every fiber of her being. For two cents, she would throw herself at him and let nature take its course.

But her pride got in the way. She was damned if she would let him think she was using sex to win him over. Either he trusted her, or he didn't.

Her mood plummeted. She had gone from fear of rejection upon her arrival to joy at seeing him again to disappointment that he wasn't prepared to believe her story.

"I'll try to stay out of your way," she said. Gavin's antagonism laced with unwilling arousal was insulting.

He folded his arms across his chest. "I doubt that will solve anything." He paused, frowning. "What would you say if I told you I believe you about the baby?"

"The baby is real," she said, deliberately misunderstanding him. "You don't have to believe me."

"You know that's not what I meant. This isn't a joke, Cass."

She inhaled sharply. "Believe me, I know that. I'm scared spitless."

His expression tautened. "Is that how you really feel?"

She hadn't meant to reveal weakness to him. "This isn't what I wanted…what I planned for. My life has run off the rails in one big, dramatic train wreck. I don't know anything at all about kids."

"I think it will come naturally."

"That's a myth perpetuated by sappy commercials and greeting cards. Babies poop all the time and scream for no reason. They're impossible to understand, and from what I can tell, their entire raison d'être is to drive otherwise functional adults to the brink of insanity."

"Have you thought about giving the child up for adoption?"

His face was a mask. She had no clue where he stood on the matter. But hearing the option spoken aloud made her realize one thing beyond any doubt. "No. He or she, poor little kid, is my flesh and blood. For better or worse. I may suck at this, but I want to be the best mom I can be."

His expression softened, and for a moment she thought she saw admiration in his gaze. "I'll help you any way I can…even if I'm not the father."

"Quit saying that," she yelled. "You *are* the father." Suddenly, several weeks' worth of anxiety and fear caught up with her. Though she scorned women who manipulated men with emotion, she was completely unable to stem the flow of salty tears and the ugly, gasping sobs that shuddered through her chest and left her raw.

Her hands were over her face, so she didn't see him come close.

"Shh," he said, gathering her into his arms. "You'll upset the baby. Everything is going to be okay. I promise."

His quiet support only made her cry harder. She hated feeling so desperately inadequate. All her life she had been the A student, the perfect daughter, the kid other kids' parents wanted their offspring to emulate.

She'd had a plan, and she'd worked hard to attain it. But now she'd lost her dream job, her home and her father's blessing. And in the process gained a responsibility for which she was definitely unprepared.

This was what happened when you broke the rules. Some people were able to pull it off without consequences. But not Cass. She should never have believed she could walk on the wild side with impunity.

Resting her cheek against Gavin's hard shoulder, her arms around his waist, she inhaled a deep breath and let it out slowly. He smelled the same as he had the night they met. A mix of aftershave and warm masculine skin and wildly erotic pheromones.

If he would hold her like this forever, she might try to squeeze out a few more tears. But the cataclysm had run its course. When she was reduced to sniffing and wiping her nose on the back of her hand, Gavin fished in his pocket for a soft cotton handkerchief, handing it to her without comment. The cloth was still warm from being close to his body.

He brushed the hair from her face. "You okay now, Cass?"

She sighed. "As okay as I can be. Nine months is a long time to be in limbo."

"Don't exaggerate," he said, eyes dancing with humor. "Surely it's only seven now."

"Easy for you to say," she muttered. "You're not the one who's going to swell up like a cow and have heartburn and need to pee constantly and—"

He put his hand over her mouth, halting her litany of dismay. Kissing her forehead, he rested his chin on top of her head. "You're going to be the most beautiful pregnant woman the world has ever seen. Men are going to stop in the street to stare at your gorgeous breasts. And women everywhere will sigh in envy at your maternal glow."

At last she chuckled. A weak laugh, but a laugh nevertheless. "You are so full of it."

"I call 'em as I see 'em."

"I'll go now," she said, pulling free of his embrace though she would gladly have stayed there forever.

"You don't have to. You can stay and watch me work."

"As lovely as that sounds, I'll pass. What is it you do anyway?"

"My cyber defense company is called The Silver Eye. I access high-end clients' servers remotely and try to breach them. When I succeed, I share the results and together we work toward a way to shore up their privacy and security."

"You must be awfully smart."

"It's a longtime hobby of mine. The fact that I was able to make a business out of it was a bonus." He glanced at his high-tech equipment and then back at Cassidy again. "What if I take you up to the hotel for dinner? China and candlelight and real linen tablecloths. You'll love it."

"It does sound nice."

"Then it's settled."

She handed him his soggy handkerchief. "What time?"

He took it with a grimace. "My mother usually arrives around seven. We'll eat with her if you don't mind. She chews my tail if I don't show up at least once a week... and I'm overdue."

"Your mother?" The words came out on a squeak of incredulity.

He shrugged. "I'll introduce you as an out-of-town friend. Your pregnancy is no one's business but ours at the moment."

"I've wondered when I'll start to show."

"Is there a formula for that?"

"Not really. It depends mostly on body type. And I've been sick so much I've actually lost weight."

"I'll make you a milk shake tonight before bed. We'll fatten you up in no time."

"Every girl's dream," she said, shaking her head at his cluelessness.

Gavin's gaze warmed to intimacy. "Most men I know like curves on their women…something to hold on to. A soft place to rest."

"For a computer geek you surely have a poetic turn of phrase."

"Maybe you inspire me."

They stood there in silence, each weighing the other's motives. In his eyes she saw the need to protect himself with emotional distance. But his body language spoke a different dialect. Already, he had touched her, comforted her, imprinted himself on her skin.

The only thing he hadn't done was kiss her. The omission seemed glaring. And regrettable.

Going up on tiptoe before she could change her mind, she captured his mouth with hers, pressing a kiss gently against his firm masculine lips. With her tongue she teased the seam until he inhaled sharply and opened to her, letting her in.

She was under no illusions. Her awkward, inexperienced seduction was neither graceful nor polished. But it did the job. Gavin growled deep in his chest and captured her nape in one big hand, pulling her close against his chest, shoving one hard thigh between hers.

"You're a brat," he muttered. But since his erection throbbed against the cleft between her legs, she didn't put much stock in his criticism.

"I've missed you," she whispered, arching her back so she could press her body even closer to his. "I didn't want to, but I did."

He nibbled a sensitive spot beneath her ear, making her squirm. "Why didn't you want to miss me?"

"I had plans to take over the world. To *be* somebody. You were a temptation I had to resist."

"Is that why you walked out of my hotel room?"

The trace of masculine pique in the sharp words told her he had been wounded by her defection. In the next second, she actually felt the change in him. The walls going up. The defenses snapping into place. Kissing her made him vulnerable, and that was the last thing in the world a man like Gavin Kavanagh wanted to feel.

"It seemed like the thing to do at the time," she said, hoping he'd understand.

"And once I was gone, how long did it take you to find another man to take my place?"

After a split second of shocked silence, she backed away sharply, tears springing to her eyes. "You're cruel and hateful and I don't know why I came here."

He scowled. "Maybe you couldn't stay away from me. Maybe there's no baby at all. Maybe that was a ploy to get into my house."

Even knowing he was fighting an attraction he didn't want, the accusation hit its mark. "Go to hell," she said, her chest heaving in wretched hurt and anger. "I don't even like you."

"Yeah," he said, his jaw rigid and his eyes stormy. "I don't like you, either."

Eight

Gavin wasn't worth a damn after that. How in the devil was he supposed to carry on with business as usual when the siren who had lured him onto the rocks in Vegas presently occupied a bedroom right down the hall?

Even worse, now that he had tasted her again, he hadn't a snowball's chance in hell of pretending he didn't want her. The need was like a tropical disease, striking without warning long after he had left the neon jungle. One look at her sweet face and mischievous eyes, and he was a goner.

Once again he allowed himself to consider the possibility that he had planted a child in her womb. *Dear God.* He should be pissed and angry and worried, but all he could latch on to was an emotion that felt a lot like euphoria. A baby. Was it possible?

He sat down hard in his chair and stared at the laptop readout in front of him. It might as well have been written in Sanskrit. The words and symbols danced across the screen, mocking his lack of comprehension. He was a man who could work for hours and never lose focus or concentration. His brain thrived on difficult puzzles.

But never had he faced a situation like this. For a moment, he saw his younger self behind bars, his fate and his reputation hanging in the balance. He'd felt utterly lost and alone.

Was he walking into another trap? Cassidy Corelli was not mentally ill. She had no need of his family's money. Yet still his unease remained. He kept going back to that night in Vegas. Why had he responded to her so viscerally? Why did she set him on fire? Not being able to understand his reactions made him uneasy. Why did a young, attractive woman wait so long to experiment with sex? And why choose a stranger?

He wasn't a whimsical man. He dealt in hard numbers and immutable equations. Over the past year or so he'd watched his brothers fall in love. In every instance, he could say without a doubt that his siblings had found mates who were perfect for them. Dylan and Aidan had reconnected with women from their pasts. Liam had discovered a female who didn't let him take life too seriously.

None of them had initiated relationships based on a one-night stand and an accidental pregnancy.

Gavin had taken several psychology classes in school. Freud would say that there *were no* accidents. That perhaps unconsciously, Gavin knew when he made love to Cass in the tub that he'd forgotten birth control and didn't care.

Was it true? Had Gavin wittingly contributed to the current situation? Or was Cassidy using that omission to coax him into believing that she carried his child?

What would have happened if he hadn't had a plane to catch that morning? Would Cassidy have stayed in his bed? From all he could tell, she was ambitious and determined to pursue her goals. He couldn't fault her for that. It was one thing they had in common.

But when she walked out of his hotel room that day, had she felt even a fillip of remorse for not saying goodbye? Or regret that she wouldn't see Gavin again?

He didn't claim to understand the fairer sex. They were

complicated and mercurial and no two were alike. How was a man ever supposed to gain the upper hand?

In the current situation, however, Gavin was determined not to let himself be swayed by physical attraction. Keeping his distance from Cassidy was a matter of self-preservation. Even if the baby *was* his, there were numerous hurdles ahead.

Did he honestly want to consider a shotgun marriage to repair her relationship with her father and give the baby Gavin's name? What chance did they have under those circumstances? Even the best of marriages failed at an alarming rate. He and Cass would be handicapped from the start. She would no doubt end up resenting him and the baby for destroying her dreams of working side by side with her father. And Gavin would always wonder if he was a means to an end.

He was tempted to believe every word she spoke, wanted to quite desperately, in fact. But if he dismissed his doubts and took her to bed again, what then?

Cassidy Corelli troubled him. He was vulnerable where she was concerned. And vulnerability was the enemy of control. The incident when he was in college had taught him to build a wall around his emotions.

If he were going to be able to navigate these next few weeks, then he had to stay away from her. No touching, no kissing and certainly no sex. He would make that very clear.

Convincing Cassidy was one thing. Convincing himself was going to be a whole lot more difficult...

Cassidy unpacked her things and tucked them into the drawers of a beautiful armoire. Gavin's home was sophisticated and lovely, not at all what she had expected when she tracked him down at the end of a private mountain road.

Maybe she had been expecting a masculine cabin with hunting trophies on the wall or a cluttered residence with big-screen TVs and recliners and pizza boxes stacked high.

The truth pointed out how little she knew about him. He was a deep river with strong undercurrents. His home reflected his love for beauty and his predilection for solitude. High ceilings, arched doorways and large windows created pleasing spaces that radiated tranquility and offered peace and the chance for reflection.

Curled up on a cushioned bay window seat, she looked out into the forest. It was the kind of scene where unicorns and centaurs might wander by. Or even a knight on a fiery steed.

As a young girl Cassidy had lost herself in books. Because her father—in his grief—had removed all pictures of Cass's mother from the house, Cassidy had often daydreamed about her mom. She had imagined the two of them weaving daisy chains and playing with puppies and stretching out on a quilt to watch cloud pictures in the sky.

Already, she found herself making lists of things she wanted to do with her baby. Books they would read together. Songs they would sing. Games they would play. God willing, her child would never have to grow up without a mother's love.

It scared her, though, to think about giving up her dreams and her career. Did she really have to? Was there a way to have it all?

And what about Gavin? Would he ever be as determined as she was to give their little one a perfect childhood? Even as she spun dreams, she acknowledged wryly that parenting was not going to be all rainbows and lullabies. It would be hard work...and at times unrewarding.

Her body was changing. Soon the evidence would be impossible to hide. What was Gavin thinking? Could he trust her without the test? Did he have any feelings for her at all? Or was she no more than an unpleasant disruption of his ordered life?

She would stay only until she had a chance to figure things out. And she would do her best to keep her distance as long as she shared Gavin's home.

When it was time, she dressed carefully for dinner. If she was going to meet her child's paternal relatives, she wanted to make a good impression...even if they had no clue what was going on.

The dress she had worn for travel was wrinkled, so she picked a sleeveless boat-necked top in black lace and paired it with a multicolored above-the-knee skirt in flirty silk. Strappy gold sandals made the look a bit dressier. The elastic waist guaranteed comfort if dinner didn't settle well.

She was ready and waiting when Gavin knocked on her door at six-thirty.

His eyes widened when he saw her. She saw the muscles in his throat work. But he didn't comment on her appearance. "Ready to go?" he asked gruffly.

She nodded, following him out into the hallway. He had shaved recently. The scent of lime tickled her nose in a pleasing fashion. His broad shoulders stretched the seams of a navy sport coat. The jacket, teamed with dark khakis and an open-necked white shirt, made him look like an ad for the successful young entrepreneur.

It was hard not to drool. She found herself wanting to strip away the trappings of conventional society and have him naked and all to herself for at least a week. Maybe then she would know where she stood.

While she was in her room dressing, Gavin had brought his car around from the garage in back of the house. Parked beside her nondescript rental was a sleek, fire-engine-red Porsche convertible, the top already stowed away.

She pulled up short. "Wow. This is yours?"

"Well, I didn't steal it if that's what you mean."

Ignoring his sarcasm, she ran a hand over the sleek hood. "I am *so* jealous," she breathed, reverently completing a circuit around the stunning vehicle. "*This* is what we should have had for our desert drive. I'm getting excited just looking at it."

Gavin had a funny look on his face. "I'm glad you approve."

"May I drive?" She looked at him beseechingly, her fingers itching to touch the controls.

He shook his head. "No, Cass. These mountain roads aren't like your straight desert highways. And this is a lot of car to handle."

She faced him toe to toe. "Please? Pretty, please? I'll be as careful as an old lady on her way to church."

They were so close she could feel the heat of his body. That heat brought back a lot of memories. They weren't touching, not at all. But they might as well have been. Arousal bloomed hot and vicious, making her catch her breath. When she would have backed away, Gavin took her wrist, his thumb pressed firmly against her wildly racing pulse.

"If it means that much to you, then okay. You can drive." The words were husky, as though his throat was as constricted as hers. "But keep it under thirty-five."

"Yes, Gavin," she said meekly.

His snort of laughter told her he wasn't fooled by her docility.

As she slid behind the wheel, Gavin went to the passenger side and sat down, handing her the key fob. When she started the engine, she felt the power vibrate through her veins. She closed her eyes for a moment, enjoying the sensation.

Her companion tapped her on the cheek. "Hello in there. Do you think we could get this party started?"

She shot him a look. "You're so impatient." Stroking the dashboard, she sighed. "This is one sexy car. It deserves to be appreciated."

"Appreciate it on your own time. I'm starving."

Gavin liked his car. A lot. But it took on a whole new persona with Cassidy behind the wheel. Her face was a study in delight. She showed no hesitance at all in backing around and sending the car hurtling down the driveway. When Gavin grabbed the door handle instinctively, she laughed out loud.

If Cassidy thought his car was sexy, that was nothing compared to how he regarded the whole experience from the passenger seat. Watching her drive his Porsche was almost as good as taking her hard and fast and hearing her cry out when he made her come.

Perhaps dinner en famille was not the best idea he'd ever had. What would she say if he asked her to turn around and go back to his house?

He never had the chance to find out. They arrived at the Silver Beeches Lodge in no time at all. Cassidy eyed the elegant hotel with appreciation. "Fancy," she said, climbing out of the car.

"It's the family business. My oldest brother, Liam, and our mother, Maeve, keep it filled to capacity. Don't be surprised if you bump into a movie star or a politician."

"I get the impression that your family owns a big chunk of the town."

He took her arm as they climbed the wide, shallow front steps. "Kavanagh ancestors built the town of Silver Glen. So in a way, yes. But it has expanded over the years."

"But hasn't lost its alpine charm."

"That's the idea. The business owners want to attract a certain clientele, so the shops are high-end and the paparazzi aren't welcome."

In the grand lobby of the hotel they ran into Conor. Gavin introduced Cassidy to his younger brother and watched as Cass dazzled him, as well. Conor looked gobsmacked. Since Conor had a certain reputation with the ladies, that was saying a lot.

Cassidy bubbled over with enthusiasm, giving Conor a quick blow-by-blow of driving the Porsche.

Conor looked over at Gavin with a raised eyebrow. "You let her drive your precious car? Damn it, man. You won't even let me *think* about driving it."

Gavin cuffed Conor on the back of the head. "Cass is a lot cuter than you are. Buy your own damn car."

The brothers squabbled amicably as they flanked Cass arm in arm and headed for the hotel dining room. The obsequious maître d' unbent enough to offer a smile as he led them across the floor to where Maeve Kavanagh was already seated at a table for four.

Maeve stood and greeted both of her sons with a kiss. "You've made an old woman very happy. I've been looking forward to this all day."

Given that Maeve was a vibrant woman in her early sixties, neither Gavin nor Conor paid much attention to her theatrics. Cassidy, however, blanched. "Oh, I'm so sorry. I shouldn't be intruding on family time."

Maeve had the grace to look abashed and backpedaled quickly. "I was thrilled when Gavin told me he was bringing a guest, my dear." Once everyone was seated, Maeve continued. "I love to see my boys, but we get overloaded with testosterone around here. It's a treat to have another woman at the table. Where are you from, Cassidy?"

Cassidy glanced at Gavin quickly, but answered easily

enough. "I met your son when he was in Vegas for a conference. My father owns a large casino there."

"I see."

Gavin could practically feel the wheels turning in his mother's head. She lived for matchmaking. Gavin could have hidden Cassidy away indefinitely, but by trotting her out at the first opportunity, he was hoping to demonstrate that he had nothing to hide.

When Conor reached for a second roll, his mother tapped his hand sharply. "You'll ruin your dinner. Chef has prepared something special for us."

Gavin grinned widely, glad to have his sibling around to deflect some of the maternal radar. Though all of Maeve's seven sons were grown with lives and careers of their own, Gavin's mother saw no reason to let them off the hook if she thought they were making mistakes, large or small.

"Tell me, Cassidy," his mother said. "What do you do for a living?"

Cass sat primly, her spine rigid as she answered. "I recently finished a business degree. My plan all along has been to step up beside my father in the family business."

Gavin smiled at his mother. "You and Cass have a lot in common. Both of you are astute businesswomen."

Maeve leaned conspiratorially in Cassidy's direction. "Beware compliments from a Kavanagh male, my dear. There's usually a hidden agenda."

"I'm not a bit surprised." Cassidy gave Gavin a look that made him squirm.

Fortunately, the server arrived with Caesar salads, and the conversation drifted to less volatile subjects. Cassidy seemed hungry, which Gavin took as a good sign. She'd told him she usually felt better later in the day, so he hoped she would enjoy tonight's meal.

"What are we having, Mom? You mentioned a chef special?"

"You'll see," Maeve said with a smile. "But let's just say he had it flown in this morning from Prince Edward Island, so it's fresh and wonderful."

When the salad plates had been cleared away, the server returned, bearing a large silver tray. He deposited it carefully in the center of the table with a flourish. "Colville Bay oysters. Enjoy!"

Maeve thanked the man. Conor whistled in delight. Gavin felt a sharp pang of hunger and couldn't wait to dig in.

Cassidy, however, had a far different reaction. She jumped to her feet, nearly overturning her chair. Her face turned an alarming shade of green, and her eyes filled with panic. "Excuse me, please."

In the wake of her abrupt departure, Gavin felt two sets of eyes on him. "I'll go see if she's okay," he said, feeling his throat flush with embarrassment and anxiety.

Maeve laid a hand on his arm, her gaze thoughtful but kind. "She's probably in the ladies' room. I'll check on her. You two boys eat. But save some for me."

Conor rubbed his chin. "Anything you want to tell me, bro?"

Gavin stared at the mucous-like crustacean and felt his own stomach flip-flop. "Nothing," he said. "Nothing at all."

Nine

Cassidy hunched over the commode, dry-heaving. If she had ever been this miserable, she couldn't remember. But when she opened the door of the stall and found Maeve Kavanagh sitting in a small chair at the ornate vanity, her stomach plummeted even farther.

"Mrs. Kavanagh. I didn't hear you come in."

Gavin's elegant mother, her auburn chignon only slightly threaded with gray, smiled gently. "Are you pregnant, dear?"

Cassidy swallowed hard and tried not to think about oysters. "No, ma'am. Of course not."

Maeve shook her head. "I'm not completely oblivious to the fact that my sons have sex lives. I choose not to dwell on the subject, but I am not naive. Gavin has never brought a girl home before."

"He didn't bring me, either. I showed up at his house for a visit, that's all."

"And that explains why you rushed from the dinner table?"

"I'm sorry. I didn't mean to be rude." Cassidy was disheveled and ill and upset, but she couldn't fault Maeve's concern for her son. "I may be coming down with something. You probably shouldn't be near me."

Maeve grinned, taking fifteen years off her age. "Are you carrying Gavin's child?"

"No. Really."

"Your commitment to the lie is impressive, but I can do this all night. Tell me, honey. Tell me the truth."

Cassidy's legs lost their starch and she sank onto an ottoman that matched the decor. "Okay. Yes. I'm pregnant."

"And is Gavin the father?"

"Yes. But he doesn't think so...or to be exact, he's not sure. He wants a paternity test."

Maeve winced. "How old are you, Cassidy?"

"Twenty-three."

"And did you want to become pregnant?"

"No, ma'am. Not at all. But now that I am, I'm going to do everything in my power to take care of this baby."

"And what do your parents think about all this?"

"My mother died when I was very young. My father is furious."

"Poor dear." Gavin's mother shook her head. "I would like to help you, if I can."

Cassidy held out her hands. "I know you mean well, but this is something Gavin and I have to work out between us. Please don't be angry. You're very kind. But I feel disloyal enough already for telling you without Gavin's consent."

"I understand. And I won't let on that I know. But I think I can shed some light on my son's attitude. Why don't you come to tea with me tomorrow? Here at the hotel. We can get to know each other."

"I'm pretty sure Gavin wouldn't like that."

"He brought you here for dinner tonight, didn't he? He may not be willing to admit yet that he's going to be a father, but deep down I'd say he acknowledges the truth."

"There are things you don't know," Cassidy said. Like

the fact that she and Gavin had been impetuous and foolish in the midst of a night of wild, crazy sex.

"I could say the same. I'll expect you tomorrow, Cassidy. Don't disappointment me."

By mutual consent the two women returned to the dining room. Cassidy was relieved to see that the oysters had disappeared. In their place were four servings of innocuous chicken piccata with fresh asparagus and brown rice. The scent actually made her stomach growl in a good way, something she thought was a statistical impossibility on this particular occasion.

As the men stood and helped the ladies to be seated, Gavin gave her a searching look. She smiled weakly. "Sorry about that." What else could she say? To attempt any sort of explanation would only make matters worse.

Fortunately, Maeve took over the conversation, directing the attention away from Cassidy. "Tell us about your trip, Conor."

Gavin jumped in eagerly, clearly happy to add to the diversion. "I haven't seen you since you got back."

Conor, too, seemed content to oblige. "I had a great time."

"Where did you go?" Cassidy asked.

"Switzerland. Lucerne to be exact. I was one of five judges in a junior alpine skiing event."

Gavin passed Cassidy the basket of homemade rolls. "Conor used to ski competitively. Now he runs the ski resort here in Silver Glen."

"Did you ever ski for the US?" she asked, studying the physical similarities between Gavin and his brother. Both men were muscular and fit, but Conor was a bit taller and leaner.

Conor shook his head. "I thought about it, of course. But I ski for the love of it…and sometimes competition gets in the way. I did make the US team as a sixteen-year-old, but I blew out my knee before I had a chance to take it all the way."

"I'm impressed," Cassidy said. "I've been known to fall off a bicycle. Sports were never my thing. I'm more of a bookworm, I guess."

Conor leaned forward, enthusiasm on his face. "I bet I could teach you to ski. We have a great bunny slope, and once you build up your confidence, you'd be surprised how much you'll enjoy it."

"I don't think so." Gavin's abrupt comment drew three confused stares.

Cassidy kicked him under the table. "What Gavin means is that I'm probably a hopeless cause. And I won't be around long enough for lessons. But it's sweet of you to offer."

Apparently Gavin thought learning to ski was not on the list of approved activities for expectant mothers. But if he wasn't even willing to believe that he was the father of her baby, she sure as heck wasn't going to take his advice on what she could and could not do.

Over dessert, Cassidy's energy level plummeted. Suddenly it was all she could do to keep her eyes open.

Gavin noticed right away and made their excuses. As everyone stood, Conor and Maeve gave Cassidy a hug. Maeve patted Cassidy's arm. "Don't forget our teatime tomorrow."

"I won't," Cassidy said, wincing inwardly.

As they left the hotel, Gavin took her arm. "Do you want the top up?" he asked. "It will be cool now that the sun has set."

In the mountains, even a warm spring day turned chilly after dark. "No," she said. The valet had the car waiting.

As Cassidy slid into the passenger seat, she leaned back and sighed. "I have my scarf. And I want to see the stars."

Gavin drove home on a slightly different route than the one they had taken earlier. At a pull-off overlooking Silver Glen, he stopped the car. Below them, the little town looked like a postcard, serene and beautiful.

"You're lucky to live here," Cassidy said. "I love the desert and the excitement of Vegas, but this is charming."

"It's home," he said.

The laconic response was all she was going to get out of him. His silence seemed ominous. Her heart sank as she realized that Gavin was no closer than ever to embracing her news. Any enjoyment she had squeezed out of the evening winnowed away beneath a wave of depression.

If she could only believe he would come around to caring for her and believing her, she would take a chance and stay. But she was deeply afraid that his past had damaged his ability to love and trust anyone other than his immediate family.

Now that Maeve had guessed about the baby, things were going to be even more complicated. Gavin would no doubt believe that Cassidy had blabbed the truth against his wishes. He would see that move as an attempt to ingratiate herself with his mother.

Back at the house, she excused herself and said goodnight. She didn't realize Gavin had followed her until he appeared in the doorway to her bedroom, a scowl on his face.

"What are you doing?" he asked, the words harsh.

She shrugged, stepping out of her shoes and wiggling her toes in the carpet. "What does it look like? I'm packing. There's no reason for me to stay after I have tea with your mother tomorrow. I came here to give you the news face-to-face, and I've done that. When the baby comes, you can give me the name of a lab you trust, and I'll show up when and where I need to."

"I told you I'd let you stay for a while."

She faced him bravely, hurt by his deliberate aloofness, but unable to find a way forward. "It's better if I go home."

"You can't go home, remember? Your father kicked you out."

"I have friends. I'm sure one of them will take me in."

"Male or female?"

Her temper flared. "Does it matter?"

On Gavin's face she saw a mix of emotions that was impossible to decipher. The only one she recognized clearly was hunger. He didn't *want* to want her, but he did. His trousers tented unmistakably.

The clear evidence of his need should have reassured her. Instead, it made her sad. If all they had between them was lust, she might as well cut Gavin loose and make her own way.

A baby needed stability. And as for Cassidy, she needed a man who at least respected her. Not someone who thought she was laying a trap.

He took a step forward with a look in his eyes that sent a shiver of primal apprehension down her spine. "Yes," he said, the word hoarse. "It matters."

Dragging her up against his chest, he wrapped his arms around her and found her mouth with his. Yearning. Excitement. An intimate knowledge of what it felt like to be possessed by this man. All those things made her melt against him despite the antagonism between them.

They might be at odds over her pregnancy, but this one thing hadn't changed.

Gavin held her firmly, his kisses coaxing and insistent. His body was telling her something he wasn't ready to admit. She was made for him and vice versa. It was as if the universe had picked out two people with the best possible sexual compatibility and tossed them together to see what would happen.

He nuzzled the side of her neck, making her squirm, breathless and wanting. "Let me go," she said.

The fact that she wrapped her arms around his neck tightly probably negated the demand.

Gavin walked her toward the bed. "You're already pregnant," he said. "It's not like we're going to make it worse."

She laughed, though it wasn't really funny. "If that's your pickup line, it sucks."

He bit her earlobe. "You'll have to forgive me. I may not be in possession of my right mind. Something about you makes me insane."

When they fell together onto the bed, it was clumsy and painful and altogether wonderful. His elbow whacked her shoulder. Her fingers ripped at his buttons. He dragged her top off over her head. In some small corner of her brain she knew she should stop him. But she couldn't bear to do it. At least this was honest. A need for a need. Two people giving and receiving pleasure.

If her heart broke in the meantime, surely it was worth the price.

He paused to stare at her bare chest, his gaze hot. "Your body is changing already," he said. The words held a note of wonder. When he cupped the sides of her breasts with both hands and gently pushed them together, a shock of heat stroked through her center, leaving her breathless.

"They've been swollen. And tender."

He brushed a nipple reverently. "Will it hurt if I taste them?"

"No." She was stunned that she could speak that single syllable. His question sent her body into a shuddering spi-

ral of blissful anticipation. When he suckled gently, her
sensitive flesh beaded tightly in his mouth.

"Gavin..." It was a whisper, a prayer.

He looked up at her, his head propped on his hand.
"Too much?"

"Not enough."

His feral smile should have warned her. Abandoning
his project for a moment, he shoved her skirt to her waist
and stripped away her satin underpants. The cool air on
her overheated skin added a layer of pleasure.

He had already shrugged out of his mangled shirt and
was bare from the waist up. The bronzed chest sculpted
with sleek muscles revealed both his physical capabilities
and his masculinity.

Beside him she felt small and pale and helpless. That
last adjective spooked her. She'd never leaned on anyone
in her life. But now she was making decisions for two.
Knowing that Gavin was around to stumble through this
experience with her would make things so much easier.

When he touched her between her thighs and teased her
with a fingertip, she gave up rational thought. At the same
moment, he returned to her breasts, his lips and teeth closing over first one tip and then the other. The dual stimula-
tion shot her over the edge of a blinding orgasm.

Gavin didn't wait for an engraved invitation. He left her
only long enough to shed his pants and boxers and shoes
before wedging his hips between her open thighs and po-
sitioning his firm length at her center. "I've dreamed about
this," he muttered. The words were barely audible...as if
they had been dragged from him unawares.

She didn't know what to say in return, so she simply
held him. Already her body recognized him as its mate.
Her sex welcomed his eagerly, sealing the bond that was

physical, but for her even more. A great deal more. She was only now beginning to understand how much.

Gavin braced his hands beside her shoulders, his strong hips thrusting powerfully, his hard shaft filling her until her womb ached. For Cassidy it was a revelation.

In Las Vegas, she had not analyzed too carefully why she had met Gavin and wanted him desperately. Now, hazily, she understood that her soul had recognized him instantly as *the one*. No other man had ever affected her that way. She was beginning to think no other man ever would.

As his skin heated, he smelled of sex and spicy aftershave. Even blindfolded, she would know him now. She lifted into his thrusts, making him groan, feeding her own pleasure.

Her second climax climbed lazily, hitting every spot along the way, rolling over her like a tide of molten honey. She bit her lip hard enough to draw blood when it caught her by surprise. As she arched beneath him, he came as well, filling her with his release.

When it was done, they each breathed heavily. Though it was dark outside, the room was almost too bright. The overhead fixture beamed down on them. Cassidy was bashful suddenly, having no idea what Gavin was thinking. Without speaking, she scooted to the bathroom, washed up and donned the robe on the back of the door. It was thick and comfy and emblazoned with the logo of the Silver Beeches Lodge.

When she returned to the bedroom, Gavin sat with his back against her headboard. He had turned off all the lights except for a small table lamp, thus making it hard to read his expression.

Courageously, she tossed back the covers and sat beside him, unsure of the postcoital etiquette. "Now what?" she asked, her throat tight.

"I guess that's up to you. I'm willing to let you stay until the baby is born. But I think it would be best if we not repeat—" He stopped suddenly.

"You're saying we shouldn't have sex." The words were like sharp stones in her chest.

"Correct."

"You came to my room. Not the other way around."

His jaw was granite. Since they were seated hip to hip, she couldn't look at his face full-on, but he radiated strong emotion. "That was a miscalculation on my part. It won't happen again."

"Why?" She put her pride on the line, aching to get at the truth.

"Isn't it obvious?"

"Not to me," she said quietly.

"We aren't a couple, Cassidy. We have a tenuous connection at best. Even if the baby turns out to be mine, it doesn't mean we have a future."

"You think that's what I'm here for?"

"You said your father told you to get married and have babies. And you've spent your whole life working to please him."

She was insulted and ashamed and pissed. "There are any number of men who would be happy to put a ring on my finger, baby or no baby. I don't need your charity, Gavin."

"How's your cousin doing?"

The odd question caught her off guard. And deflated her anger effectively. "He's fine. The state renewed his license and backdated it to the expiration date of the old one, so his boss is happy."

Gavin got to his feet and wrapped the sheet around

his waist. But not before she got an eyeful of his considerable assets. He knotted the swath of cotton and stared at her, eyes narrowed, hands on hips. "Are you telling me that when we stood in front of him and repeated marriage vows, he was a legal celebrant for the state of Nevada?"

Suddenly, she saw where his mind was going. "Yes. But don't jump to conclusions, Gavin. You didn't sign anything. There was no license. We were only goofing around. I didn't trick you into marrying me. Your conspiracy theories are ridiculous. And you have far too high an opinion of yourself. We had a fling. That's all."

"Why did you take me to the chapel that night?"

"For exactly the reasons I told you. Robbie's my favorite cousin. I promised I would stop by and see him that night. And I thought it would be fun for you to get a taste of the whole Vegas experience." She paused. "Listen, Gavin. I have a baby to think about now. So as much fun as it is to burn up the sheets with you, it's not my priority. I'm going to go home and get a job and an apartment. One of the other casinos will hire me to work in their offices. When the baby comes, I'll be in touch."

He glanced at her open suitcase on the floor. "I have a vested interest in your pregnancy. I want you close by to keep an eye on you."

"In view of your cynical suspicions, I don't give a damn what you want. Besides, are you really prepared to attend doctor's appointments and childbirth classes?"

He blanched. "Yes to the first…no to the second. I'm calling for a truce for the next six-plus months. It's in the baby's best interests."

Gavin was everything she wanted and everything she needed. But he wasn't hers to keep. "Maybe so," she said. "But what if we kill each other in the meantime?"

Ten

The fabulous sex should have relaxed Gavin and sent him off to dreamland, but it had the opposite effect. He tossed and turned for hours, unable to get the images of Cass out of his head.

He was infatuated with her. And that was dangerous. In other circumstances, he would simply screw her until he got her out of his system. But this pregnancy thing brought other factors into play.

At three, he got up and turned on the television. As he stared at a rerun of a 1950s sitcom, he asked himself the question he'd been avoiding. *Was* he willing to be a father to Cass's baby?

Perhaps the more pressing question was, could he let her go if the baby *wasn't* his? Right now, he had a legitimate claim, based on her insistence that he was the only man with whom she'd been intimate.

He wanted to believe her. But everything about that night in Vegas seemed surreal. The fight in the alley. The drive out in the desert. Coaching Robbie at the wedding chapel. Even the incredible sex.

Couples were supposed to have to learn each other's likes and dislikes before reaching that kind of mountaintop. Hell, he would give each and every time he and Cass had done it a best-in-show ribbon.

He took his phone and clicked on the photo icon. Scrolling back only a few spots, he found the selfie Cassidy had insisted they take in the chapel. Gavin studied the image. Though he wasn't smiling in the picture, something about his posture was relaxed. Cassidy radiated fun and happiness as she kissed his chin.

The photograph was more fiction than documentary. The real Gavin was neither spontaneous nor reckless. Even his kindest critic wouldn't describe him as fun-loving. He worked hard. He cared about his family. He kept up with his responsibilities.

But he wasn't impulsive. He wasn't lighthearted. He wasn't a match for Cassidy Corelli.

At last accepting the fact that he wasn't going to sleep, he headed for his office. He'd pay for it tomorrow, but at least he could lose himself in work and try to forget the feel of Cass's soft skin beneath his fingertips.

Cassidy dreamed that night. Brilliant, vivid dreams in full color. When she got up to go to the bathroom, she replayed every part so she could remember it in the morning. The sequence that left her shaky and confused was the one where she and Gavin stood beneath a white trellis woven with pink roses. There was no baby in sight...only Gavin in a tux and Cassidy in a sexy, close-fitting white dress that clung to her every curve.

As she climbed back into bed, she fretted. What did it mean? Did she secretly not want this baby at all? Had she come to Silver Glen to find her lover, Gavin, instead of her baby's father?

The questions persisted throughout the night and were with her still next morning when she stumbled to the kitchen in search of crackers or dry toast. In hindsight, she should have made sure she had something to nibble on in her bedroom.

Praying she wouldn't bump into Gavin, she moved stealthily through the house. The faint light of dawn filtered through windows here and there. She was sick and shaky, a cold sweat dampening her forehead, as she rummaged through cabinets. When a hand touched her shoulder, she jumped a foot and cried out.

Gavin took her by the elbows and steered her to a chair at the kitchen table. "Sit," he muttered.

She rested her forehead on her crossed arms. For a bleak moment she wished she could roll back the clock to a time where she had never met Gavin…a moment when her biggest worry was whether or not she was going to get an A on her graduate thesis.

He didn't turn on the lights, and for that she was grateful. The pale early-morning sun was bad enough. Though she kept her eyes closed tightly, she was aware of him moving around the kitchen. After a few minutes her nose twitched at the smell of toast.

Gavin set a plate at her elbow. "You'll feel better if you get something in your stomach," he said. His words were gruff but not unkind. She made herself sit up, inhaling sharply when the room spun. While she concentrated on steadying the gyroscope that made her insides tumble like clothes in a dryer, Gavin finished brewing a cup of hot tea.

He loaded it with sugar and brought it to her, snagging a chair for himself and turning it backward. "Come on, honey," he cajoled. "Try a sip of the tea first."

She knew he was right. But she hated the prospect of another run to the bathroom. The fragile china was painted with a delicate Greek key design in gold and navy. Lifting the cup to her lips, she managed a taste. The tea was hot and strong, just as she liked it. When the first sip stayed down, she tried a second. Five minutes later, she started on the toast.

Gavin was amazingly patient and surprisingly intuitive. He kept quiet, content to monitor her progress from across the table. Unshaven and heavy-eyed, he was as handsome as ever. The pale yellow cotton button-down he wore was soft from multiple washings. He had rolled the sleeves to his elbows, exposing tanned forearms dusted with golden hair.

The fact that even his big manly hands turned her on was distressing.

Finally, she sighed and wrinkled her nose. "Thanks. I'm better now."

Though he'd been careful to keep physical distance between them, his smile held sympathy and admiration. "I don't know how women do it. Whoever called you the weaker sex was an idiot."

The gentle praise shored her spirits. That and the fact that he didn't seem as angry this morning.

He reached in his shirt pocket and pulled out a scrap of paper. "Here are the names of three good ob-gyns in Silver Glen. You can research them online. Let me know when you schedule the ultrasound, and I'll clear my calendar."

"Why do you work so hard?"

"You mean because I don't have to?"

"Yes."

"Why do you want to be your father's second in command?"

She pondered his question. "Fair point. If I wanted to, he'd have been happy for me to sit at home doing needlepoint or whatever the twenty-first-century equivalent is…"

"I like what I do. And it helps people. Seems to me like those are reason enough." He paused. "I have a full schedule today. Will you be okay on your own?"

"Of course. Remember that your mother has invited me to afternoon tea, so that will be nice."

He frowned. "I'm glad you didn't tell her about us last night."

"Well, I…"

He carried on, oblivious to her distress. "I know we'll have to say something sooner or later, but why cause a commotion before we have to?"

"She knows," Cass blurted out. "She guessed."

"Well, hell."

"She promised to pretend she *doesn't* know. I suppose *you* can pretend you don't know that she knows. One big happy family."

His jaw worked. "Is that supposed to make me feel guilty?"

"Not at all. You're entitled to your feelings."

"And what about you?"

"I'll get used to the idea. I really don't have much choice, now, do I?" She said it defiantly, hoping to provoke a reaction, but as usual, Gavin was not easily ruffled.

"I'll get someone to return your rental car. While you're here in Silver Glen, you can use one of mine."

"The Porsche?" she asked hopefully.

At last, his serious facade cracked. "In your dreams. You'll have to settle for a safe and sturdy Subaru."

"In other words, a *mommy* car."

"Might as well embrace your new status. From what I hear, it's a lifetime role."

"If you're trying to cheer me up, you're really bad at it."

He patted her hand and stood up. "More toast? More tea?"

"No. I'm fine. Thank you."

After carrying the dishes to the sink, he returned to the table and stood beside her, running a hand through her rumpled hair. Although she hadn't bothered to peek in a mirror this morning, she knew she must look like a bag lady.

His touch made her shiver.

"Take it one day at a time, Cass. You'll get through this."

The pronoun didn't escape her attention. *You'll* get through this. Not *we'll* get through this. Even now, and despite his hospitality, Gavin was no more open than ever to the idea that he was about to become a father.

It hurt. A lot. But since there wasn't a darn thing she could do about it, she put on a brave face. "Shall I throw something together for dinner tonight?"

"I don't need anyone to look after me, Cass. Rest. Read a book. I rarely remember to eat dinner anyway…at least not until eight or nine. I think it would be better if you didn't wait on me."

She nodded stiffly. "I understand. I suppose I'll see you when I see you." Before he could say anything else to upset her or make her feel like an interloper, she walked out of the room.

Gavin pressed his fingertips to his temples, feeling the unmistakable beginnings of a tension headache. Despite his decision to maintain an emotional distance from Cassidy, seeing her so downcast and wretched made him feel like scum.

He wanted to cuddle her and comfort her, but that would take him down a road he wasn't prepared to travel. Sex made a man stupid. He wasn't going to let himself be emotionally manipulated.

Though he worked several hours in his office, he was keenly aware of Cass's presence in his home. He spent a lot of time alone and liked it that way. Having her so close kept him off balance.

He heard the front door slam when she left to meet his mother. That in itself was disturbing. Was Maeve simply being sociable as was her habit, or did the fact that she guessed Cassidy was pregnant put her on high alert?

Doggedly, he forced himself to concentrate. Like an alcoholic counting days sober, Gavin was determined not to touch Cassidy again. Cold showers, working out in his home gym, battling Liam on the hotel's racquetball court...whatever it took, he would deny himself pleasure in exchange for knowing he was not tempted to do something stupid. He couldn't be sure, even now, that Cassidy was telling the truth. He wouldn't be duped. Not again. No matter that her smile lit up the room and her laughter soothed his soul.

The situation would become untenable if Cassidy realized how much he wanted her physically. So the solution was simple. He had to keep his wits about him, and he had to be celibate as long as she was in Silver Glen.

The prospect was unappealing at best. But he would make it work. He had to. If he let her see his weakness, she would worm her way into his ordered, solitary life. And if her claims of paternity turned out to be a hoax, he'd be screwed. It was better this way.

Cassidy found the car keys on the kitchen table with a brief note from Gavin. Apparently he couldn't even be bothered to stop by her room and drop them off. Perhaps he was afraid she would lure him into her bed like some femme fatale. Since she could count the number of times she'd had sex on one hand, his caution was ludicrous.

She dressed for her invitation to the lodge as carefully as she had the night before. Temperatures were supposed to hit the lower eighties by mid-afternoon—a heat wave for spring—so she donned a cheery sundress in poppy red and topped it with a crocheted ecru shrug. Canvas espadrilles and a straw market tote completed her ensemble.

Maeve Kavanagh met her in the hotel lobby. Gavin's mother was an impressive woman. She didn't try to dress below her age, but neither was her sense of style dowdy. Cassidy knew her hostess had been widowed many years ago. It was a marvel that some other discerning man hadn't snapped her up.

"We'll eat in my office," Maeve said, taking Cassidy's arm and steering her down a hallway that led to the back corner of the building.

Office was somewhat of a misnomer. Maeve's quarters were lovely and bright. An antique rolltop desk occupied one wall, its paper-laden surface evidence of Maeve's active role in running the lodge. But by far the largest portion of the room was given over to a feminine sitting area.

The furniture was upholstered in flowery English chintz. On a low table sat a silver coffee service. Above a gas-log fireplace, what looked to be a genuine Mary Cassatt hung proudly, its colors accenting the room's decor.

Cassidy took a wingback chair at Maeve's urging. The older woman chose a spot on the sofa just opposite her guest.

Maeve poured a cup of coffee and handed it across the table. "I forgot to ask if you are limiting caffeine. I can ring for something else."

"It's fine. I drink just enough coffee to be sociable. Otherwise, water is what keeps me going."

Maeve filled her own cup and sat back. "You're probably very wise. I grew up in a generation that mainlined this stuff. I try to keep it in check, but I'll admit to being addicted. So tell me, Cassidy," she said. "What are your addictions?"

Sex with your son seemed like an inappropriate rejoinder, so Cass reached for something more socially acceptable. "Well, I spend a great deal of time at our family's casino. I've been learning the business in hopes of becoming my father's second in command. If I have any spare time, I like to bicycle...and I get a kick out of organizing my friends' closets. I guess that makes me sound hopelessly dull."

"Not at all. Perhaps I'll let you take a crack at mine."

Cassidy let that one pass. Getting overly chummy with Gavin's mother seemed like a surefire way to get under his skin. "I think Gavin was worried about me coming here today."

Maeve eyed her over the rim of the cup. "Oh, really? How so?"

"He thanked me for not letting the cat out of the bag last night. I had to confess that you guessed that I'm pregnant."

"That must have been awkward."

"Yes, ma'am."

"I wouldn't worry about it. What you and I talk about is really none of his business."

"Are you sure about that? I think Gavin would disagree."

"Men and women usually disagree. That's what makes the battle of the sexes so much fun."

"I don't think I'm prepared to wage a war. All I want Gavin to do is trust me."

Maeve sobered. "That's not going to be easy, Cassidy. He had a terrible incident with a female when he was in college. It left him not a misogynist, but a skeptic, I suppose."

"What happened?"

"A woman accused him of rape."

Cassidy's heart sped up. "That's preposterous. Gavin is an honorable, decent man. He would never force anyone."

Maeve stared at her. "I wish his brothers and I had been so fiercely loyal. We believed him, of course. But the woman was so very convincing. There were odd moments when I wondered if Gavin saw doubt in our eyes, and it wounded him."

"You were human."

"Yes. But he was my boy. And I let him down. We all did. Gavin refused to be bailed out. When the woman's lawyer demanded a huge settlement in exchange for dropping the whole thing, I finally realized Gavin was being set up."

"How dreadful."

"Turns out, she had never even slept with Gavin. She was a patient at a mental institution in the next town. One night she and a cohort, who posed as the lawyer, slipped away. Her partner convinced her that with the money they squeezed out of an outrageous claim against an innocent man, they could run away. Gavin spent five nights behind bars before her parents tracked her down and the truth came out."

"I don't know what to say. It's so sick and cruel."

"Well, that's the point, I guess. She *was* sick. In order to find a mark at random, she spent time at the university and as luck would have it, she latched on to Gavin. It was after their first date that she made the accusation. He was blindsided."

Cassidy reeled inwardly. No wonder he was so upset to find out that he hadn't really rescued her from an attacker. And that she was a virgin. And that she had cajoled him into playing bride and groom with Robbie, the Elvis impersonator.

In his shoes, she might have been just as suspicious. Everything that had transpired between her and Gavin was innocent. But Cassidy was a stranger to him. And the crazy wonderful night they had shared could be construed as some kind of setup, particularly since she wound up pregnant. What a mess.

"I think I should probably go back to Vegas," she said, heartsick and discouraged.

Maeve disagreed. "Give him time, my dear. You each need time…time to see if you could actually make a go of this."

"I didn't come here to get a husband. I only thought Gavin should know about the baby."

"Nevertheless, something drew the two of you together when you met in Vegas. Don't underestimate the value of powerful sexual attraction. Many good marriages have started with less."

"I'm so confused."

"That's natural. I had seven babies, and every time I was pregnant, I felt as if I were wandering in a fog. Growing a human life is difficult. The process makes demands on your body, and it plays with your mind."

"Were you sick?"

"For the first three months, yes. But after that things improved. To be honest, though, I had friends who struggled with nausea the whole time. So don't be shocked if that's the case."

"Oh, goody. Something else to look forward to…in addition to heartburn and stretch marks and sleepless nights."

Maeve chuckled, her expression wry. "No one ever said being a woman is easy. But I'm here for you, Cassidy. All you have to do is ask. I want my son to be happy, and I think you're the woman to make that happen."

Eleven

Cassidy barely saw Gavin for two solid days. On the third day, she headed out the door right after lunch for her ultrasound. She had barely made it to the car, when Gavin came strolling out of the house dressed and ready to go.

She put a hand on the driver's door. "What are you doing?"

"Going with you." He took the keys from her hand and motioned her around the car. "Come on. We don't want to be late."

She stared at him, bemused. She'd put the information on a piece of paper and laid it on his dresser yesterday with no comment. She wasn't even sure if he had seen the note. Yet here he was.

They didn't talk on the way to the doctor's office. Gavin was withdrawn, and Cassidy couldn't think of any topic that wouldn't lead to trouble. The visit to the specialist was a lesson in patience. First there were papers to fill out. Then they took her back for blood work and urinalysis. Finally, they returned her to the waiting area where Gavin sat and said that someone would be with her shortly.

Shortly must have been a euphemism, because an hour elapsed from the time they arrived until the moment a harried nurse appeared to get Cassidy settled in an exam room. Gavin had insisted on going along for this leg of the journey, so Cassidy didn't quibble, especially since he stayed out in the hall while she put on a gown.

There was no seating except the doctor's rolling stool, so Gavin leaned against the wall, his hands shoved in his pockets. It was a good thing the nurse had already checked her blood pressure, because Cassidy's heart rate was through the roof.

Fortunately, the doctor appeared after only ten minutes or so. She grimaced. "I'm Doctor Mensch. Sorry for your wait. We had an unexpected delivery, and my colleague who was supposed to be on call came down with a stomach virus. We've been scrambling to cover everything." She glanced at the chart the nurse had started. "I see the date of your last period. Are you fairly regular?"

Cassidy shrugged, her cheeks turning red. "Actually, I know exactly when I got pregnant. It was just the one night." She named the month and day.

The doctor's eyebrows went up, but she didn't ask for elaboration. "In that case, it looks like you're not quite eleven weeks. Let's do an ultrasound and see how things look."

Cassidy had expected the blob of jelly on her abdomen, but the physician shook her head. "We'll get more information from a transvaginal ultrasound. It won't hurt at all." The doctor glanced at Gavin. "Are you the father?"

Gavin opened his mouth, but Cassidy rushed into the breach. "No. He's not. Just a friend." Over the doctor's bent head, Cassidy shot Gavin a stubborn look. He had refused to accept the truth. She didn't want to hear any polite lies from him now.

Though his face darkened and his eyes flashed, Gavin remained silent. His expression, however, said there would be hell to pay later.

Cassidy squeaked when the instrument was inserted. It was cold. Her hands gripped the sides of the exam table.

The older woman noticed and smiled encouragingly. "This is rarely uncomfortable. Try to relax."

Easy for her to say. It wasn't every day Cassidy saw a tiny being who might turn out to have her hair or Gavin's eyes. For some reason, the room fell silent. It wasn't as if the doc needed to concentrate. Moving a wand inside a confined space wasn't exactly rocket science.

Three sets of eyes locked on the computer screen. But Cassidy was torn. She kept an eye on Dr. Mensch, too, waiting to see a nod of approval.

When a tiny frown appeared between the doctor's eyebrows, Cassidy's heart clenched. "What is it? What's wrong?"

The ob-gyn studied the screen. "Nothing at all. Everything looks good. And based on what you told me about the date of conception, we're right on target."

"But?" Cassidy had always had a knack for reading people, and there was something the doc wasn't saying. "But what?"

Moving the wand and applying pressure here and there, the doctor finally zeroed in on one grainy image. "There. Look at that."

To Cassidy, the readout might as well have been an M.C. Escher drawing. "I see blobs and spots. Help me out here. Does the kid have two noses? An extra set of hands? You're scaring me."

The doctor smiled, her expression mischievous. "In a manner of speaking. It's twins, Cassidy. Two babies. Congratulations. You're going to be doubly blessed."

Gavin felt as if someone had punched him in the chest. It was hard enough trying to convince himself that he might have fathered one child. Now fate had anted up to two. He glanced at Cassidy. She was almost as pale as the white paper cover on the exam table.

He put a hand on her shoulder. "You okay?"

She looked up at him, panic in her eyes. "What am I going to do, Gavin?"

The doctor glanced from Cassidy to Gavin and back again. "Is there a problem?"

"No problem," Gavin said. "She's a little shell-shocked, obviously." He swallowed hard, wondering how in the heck he had arrived at this juncture in his life. "We both are. But it will all work out." He took Cass's hand in his and squeezed it, trying to convey solidarity.

The doctor gave Cassidy a tissue and helped her sit up. "We'll print out a set of photos for you to take home. I'll want to see you back here in a month. Sooner if you have any problems. You're young and very healthy. This should be a straightforward pregnancy."

When the doctor exited, Gavin exhaled. "Well, that was a surprise."

"Uh-huh." Cassidy sat on the end of the table, her hands twisting in her lap. She stared at a spot on the far wall, her gaze unfocused. His bet was that she was in shock.

He put an arm around her shoulders. "We need to go, Cass. They'll need the exam room."

When she looked up at him, her pupils were dilated. "I don't feel like I'm having twins. How can it be possible?"

"Put your clothes on. We'll discuss it in the car. I'll buy you a milk shake and we can drive over to Asheville and look at nursery furniture. They have one of those baby superstores. I went there once with Dylan when he wanted to surprise Mia with a toy box for Cora."

Cassidy was silent as she handed over her co-pay and then let him lead her out to the parking lot. She winced at the bright sunshine. When she donned sunglasses, he could no longer read her emotions.

They picked up shakes at a drive-through window, vanilla for Cass and black cherry for him. Out on the interstate, he chose an XM station that played classical music. Cassidy still hadn't uttered more than a dozen words since the doctor gave them the news.

He drove carefully, suddenly conscious as never before that he was carrying not one but three lives in his hands. As they reached the outskirts of the city, he finally asked the question that had bothered him since Cassidy arrived on his doorstep. "Cass?"

"Hmm?" She sounded sleepy.

"Is there someone you should call about today's news?"

"You mean my father?"

"No. I was thinking of any other guy who might be a daddy to your twins. Shouldn't you give someone a heads-up?"

Slowly, she removed her sunglasses and turned sideways to face him. "No," she said flatly. "You're it. Get used to the idea."

Her militant attitude didn't bother him. For the first time, he wanted to believe her without reservation. But his old biases held him back.

At the baby store, they wandered the furniture aisles. Cassidy's eyes brightened when she spotted a traditional Jenny Lind crib and changing table in solid cherry. Unlike most of the mass-produced items, this was handmade by a local North Carolina craftsman.

When she flipped the tag to look at the price, she blanched. "I can't afford this. Especially times two. We'll have to try a thrift store."

"You're kidding, right?" Her dad owned an enormous, popular casino.

Cassidy shrugged, her expression resigned. "I'm un-employed, remember? And my father canceled my credit cards. I'll need to watch my spending."

He pulled the paper tags for the various items. "I'll buy the baby furniture and put the delivery on hold until you know where you'll be living."

She grabbed his wrist. "Why would you do that? According to you, it's not your responsibility."

The words had teeth. Guilt pinched, but he wasn't quite ready to cave. He wanted to believe Cass, but this was too big a decision to make lightly. If he wrapped his head and his heart around those two little beings growing inside her and they turned out not to be his, he wouldn't be worth a damn. "Let's just say I can afford it. What good is having money if you can't make life easier for your friends?"

"Who said you and I are friends?"

He raised an eyebrow. "Don't press your luck, Cass."

"Well, in that case…" With a scowl, she started tossing stuff in the shopping cart. Crib sheets, wall hangings, burp cloths, pacifiers, a high-tech baby monitor.

The stubborn tilt to her chin said she was waiting for him to stop her. But he wanted to see how far she would go. In ten minutes, the cart was almost too heavy to push. When a precariously balanced box of diapers began to slide off, Gavin caught it and put it underneath.

"You done now?" he asked.

Cass pushed a stray curl from her forehead. She was flushed, her forehead damp with perspiration. "I'll pay you back," she said, her stormy gaze daring him to disagree.

He eyed the trove of baby paraphernalia. "You may have to work the streets of Vegas, after all, to cover this."

"That's not funny."

When he saw tears in her eyes, he suddenly remembered everything he had ever read about expectant moms and hormones. Poor Cassidy. Her whole life had been turned upside down. And this was only the beginning.

"I'm sorry. Bad joke," he said, heading for the checkout lanes. "Let's get you home so you can take a nap."

As it turned out, she slept in the car. Gavin heard her gentle snore before they had been on the road fifteen minutes. He drove slowly, in no hurry to get back to Silver Glen. As they headed up into the mountains, he pulled off at a scenic overlook and parked.

Cassidy never stirred. The tiny frown on her forehead disturbed him. Were her dreams unpleasant, or was she still mad at him?

For the first time, a novel thought occurred to him. What if he accepted the babies regardless of their parentage? Was it enough that Cassidy was their mom and Gavin wanted Cassidy?

He watched her sleep and felt a shift in his thinking. Cass wasn't the only one whose reality was changing. Like it or not...father or not...Gavin was reaping the results of his one wild night in Vegas.

It was an unexpected pleasure to be able to study her intently without her knowing. Asleep, she looked closer to eighteen or twenty than twenty-three. He was only six years older than she was, but it felt like a much wider gulf than that.

She'd been innocent when it came to physical intimacy. He still hadn't come to terms with that. If both of them had acted out of character that one crazy night, what did it say about the chances for any kind of long-lasting relationship?

No matter the difficulties and the questions, he couldn't turn his back on Cassidy. Her father had thrown her out. Gavin never would. Not unless some other man came to claim her.

Imagining that scenario hurt. A lot. The severity of

his mental reaction told him he was in far deeper than he wanted to admit.

He wanted to touch her...if only to ruffle her dark hair or straighten the shirt that had rucked up to reveal a slice of soft golden skin at her waist. The urge was almost uncontrollable.

Soon, very soon, she would start to show. When that happened, his whole family would speculate. They weren't shy about asking questions. While it was comforting to know that he and Cassidy had a circle of support when it came time for the babies to be born, one part of him wanted to hide her away and keep her for his own.

She stirred and sat up, a crease on her cheek where she had rested against the seat belt. "Sorry," she said, yawning. "I seem to keep doing that."

"It's good for you and the babies."

She paled, her eyes dark and wide. "I thought maybe I dreamed that."

"No such luck. Try to think of it as efficiency...two for the price of one."

"It's too early to joke about this," she muttered. "Somebody up there made a big goof. I'm not the maternal type. The prospect of one baby freaked me out, much less two."

"I have faith in you, Cassidy."

"Why are you being so nice to me?"

The grumpy note in her voice made him want to smile, but he held it in. "It seemed like you were having a rough day. I'm trying to be supportive."

"Unless you can push two watermelons out of your female parts, you're pretty much useless to me now."

This time he did chuckle. "Women do it every day. How bad could it be?"

"Maybe like giving a guy a mammogram on his family jewels."

He winced and held up a hand. "I stand corrected." He started the engine and backed out of the parking space. "When we get home I have a proposition for you."

Cassidy yawned and rummaged in her oversize tote for a bottle of water. "I think that was what got us into this mess. Don't you remember?"

He *did* remember. In stunning detail. And that recollection made it very difficult to be objective about Cassidy's pregnancy. Or his own role in the situation. In fact, his life would be a whole lot easier if he could erase every moment of the time he'd spent in bed with Cassidy Corelli.

Easier maybe. But not nearly as much fun.

Twelve

Back at the house, Cassidy planned to hide out in her room and try to come to terms with the soap opera that was her life. But she and Gavin were still in the driveway when her phone rang.

She muttered an unladylike word.

Gavin shot her a glance. "Who is it?"

"My father."

"Are you going to tell him about the babies? Plural?"

The phone continued to ring. "No. Not yet." She didn't want to answer, especially with Gavin listening in. Getting another lecture from her father about the need for a husband and a wedding ring was an embarrassment she'd just as soon not share. "I'll call him back in a minute."

Inside the house, she was ready to disappear when Gavin took her arm. "Not so fast. I want to show you something."

He led her down the hall where her bedroom was located. His was farther back. And across from it was a door she hadn't opened.

She came to a halt. "Are you about to show me your collection of baseball cards and workout equipment?"

His lips quirked in a half smile. "No. Those are in the garage. Take a look. I thought you could use this as a temporary nursery when the babies first arrive."

"Oh." She peeked inside and was pleasantly surprised. The room was easily fourteen by fourteen, plenty big enough for two infants. At the moment, the furnishings consisted of a set of twin beds and a bedroom suite that was probably used for guests.

Gavin leaned against the door frame. "Some of my clients like to have face-to-face consultations. I occasionally offer them a room here."

"How would that work if the house is full of babies?"

"They're tiny at first, right? We can manage. There's the Silver Beeches Lodge, of course, and also half a dozen B and Bs in town. It's not a problem."

"And I won't be here for all that long." She said it deliberately, to goad him, to get a reaction...any reaction.

For a moment, she thought she had failed. His expression was blank, closed off. But before she could blink, he reeled her into his arms and kissed her hard. The embrace left them both breathless.

Gavin brushed her cheek with the back of his hand. "One day at a time, Cass."

Her phone rang again, shattering the moment of intimacy. Same caller. "I'll take this in my room," she said, her stomach curling.

Gavin kissed her one more time, this one gentle and sweet. "Don't let him be a bully. You have options."

Cassidy had been on the line with her dad for fifteen minutes, and not once had he mentioned her pregnancy. She squelched the stab of hurt. Apparently the impetus for this call was a far more pressing concern.

"I need you to come back, right away," her father bellowed. "I've lost half a million dollars already."

Letting him ramble and bluster for several minutes, she finally got the picture. Someone had infiltrated the casino's computer systems and was siphoning money into an offshore account. Gianni Corelli had spotted the missing cash, but that was as far as he had gotten.

Cassidy was sympathetic, but she wouldn't be a doormat. "You threw me out, remember? Why can't Carlo handle this?"

Her father's volume rose two decibels. "That pup can barely even *turn on* a computer," he yelled "You're the one with the brains. Come home, Cassidy. I need you."

Interestingly, he hadn't realized he needed her until she wound up on the other side of the country. "I'll think about it, Daddy." She sensed his rage, but beneath it was fear. Her father had built a mighty empire. It must be maddening to see it threatened.

Part of her was angry that her only parent hadn't acknowledged her pregnancy at all. Or admitted that he was wrong to throw her out. Or at least shown some appreciation for her talent and her dreams for the casino. But she told herself it was just as well, because she was no closer to having any answers than when she left Vegas.

He spent another five minutes demanding her immediate presence, but Cassidy stood firm. "I'll call you tomorrow," she said. "But I make no promises." He knew what he had done. It wouldn't hurt him to spend a few hours learning to regret that he had booted his only daughter to the streets.

Over dinner prepared by Gavin's housekeeper, Cassidy told Gavin about the crisis in Las Vegas.

His forkful of lasagna stopped halfway to his mouth. "So he wasn't calling about your pregnancy…or to check on how you were feeling?"

"Never even mentioned it," she said wryly. She swallowed a bite of the garlic bread that was to die for. "But I let him know that he couldn't order me around like a child."

"Good for you."

"I need a favor," she said. The request was really rather ballsy considering all he had done so far, but he *was* her babies' father. And this request would indirectly benefit them.

Gavin took a sip of his Chianti and wiped his mouth on a napkin. "Okay." He seemed cautious but resigned.

"Do you think you could hack the casino's security protocols and help me figure out who's doing this?"

He caught on immediately. "That's brilliant. If we succeed, your father would take you back with open arms."

"That's what I was thinking." But was that truly what she wanted? She was confused and adrift. If her father changed and her goals were back on track, where did that leave her relationship with Gavin? And what about the twins? She knew she wanted to be at home with them, at least for a few years.

"Do you have the appropriate access codes?"

"If they haven't updated them. And I doubt they have. I haven't been gone that long."

"Then let's give it a try."

In Gavin's amazing office, he offered her a high-backed leather chair that matched his. She sat beside him at the console while he booted up one of his computers. One of the things she liked about him was that he wasn't scared off by her intelligence.

In college and grad school, she'd sometimes started dating a guy only to get dumped when he found out that her looks didn't equate with being a party girl. And the smart ones...the boys she would have enjoyed going out with, rarely asked her out *because* of her looks.

Gavin, on the other hand, seemed to enjoy the whole package. It made her feel good. Really good.

He pulled up a screen and glanced at her. "You ready?"

She nodded, her heart racing. What they were attempting was probably illegal...unethical at best. But the casino was part of her life, part of her birthright. She had a vested interest in seeing it succeed.

As she rattled off username and password, Gavin entered all sorts of characters and letters that looked like gibberish to her. "What are you doing?" she asked, frowning. This didn't seem like the usual log-in procedure.

"We don't want anyone to notice that we're poking around. I'm essentially camouflaging our access."

She leaned forward, fascinated by his matter-of-fact knowledge of things that were Greek to her. Soon, he pulled up a visual of the security suite. She and Gavin could see the multiple television screens that monitored everything happening in various parts of the casino. "Amazing," she whispered.

Gavin shot her a grin. "You don't have to be quiet. No one knows we're here."

She punched his arm. "Don't make fun of me."

In that moment, she realized this was the first time since she had arrived in North Carolina that she didn't feel at odds with Gavin. He was more like the man she had met in Vegas.

Who knew how long his good humor would last...

After forty-five minutes, she began to get bored. Gavin was deeply immersed in his task. But since she hadn't a clue how he was doing it, and because she had nothing to contribute at this point, she decided to bow out. "I think I'll go now."

Gavin barely acknowledged her departure.

With a sigh, she wandered down the hallway to the room he had offered as a nursery. Sitting on one of the twin beds, she tried to imagine what this space would look like with two babies in residence. Her pregnancy still didn't seem entirely real, even after seeing the evidence on an ultrasound.

What did seem *very* real were her feelings for Gavin. She cared about his opinion of her. And she wanted to be a part of his life. She might even be falling in love with him, though her mind shied away from that thought. Too much room for heartbreak.

What was she going to do? She had some big decisions to make and no road map. Even if she understood Gavin's reservations about accepting his paternity on faith, it didn't make things any easier for her. He'd told her she could stay until the babies were born, but that wasn't a viable solution, was it? If she hunkered down in his home, seeing him every day, the outcome would be inevitable. She would want to stay in his house and in his heart. It was easy to hope he might give up his doubts about her trustworthiness. Easy, but not realistic.

Given what Maeve had shared with her about Gavin's past, trust wasn't a commodity he shared easily. Perhaps even the attraction that burned so brightly between the two of them increased his misgivings.

Cassidy wanted a father for her babies, but even more than that, she wanted a man who loved her unequivocally. Once Gavin saw legal proof that the babies were his, he would do the right thing. She had no worries there. But that wasn't enough. It never would be.

She'd given her innocence to a wonderful man. But was the sexual chemistry between them a sign of something deeper? For her part, it was becoming more and more clear that the answer was yes. Gavin was smart and funny and sexy and masculine in a way that made a woman feel protected…even if she could take care of herself.

Staying in his home would almost certainly increase

the intimacy between them, with or without sex. Which would make Cassidy incredibly vulnerable to deep hurt.

She had to come up with another plan. One that didn't involve Gavin. She was a mature, well-educated woman. She could figure this out. But how could she leave Silver Glen when her heart was trapped here?

Gavin stretched and craned his neck, working out the knots from sitting too long. It hadn't been easy, but he'd done it. He knew who was stealing from Cassidy's father. Telling her was a task he'd rather not face.

Surely it could wait until morning.

He yawned as he shut everything down and prepared to head to bed. It was almost 2:00 a.m.

The house was quiet when he left his office. Some part of him wanted to make sure Cassidy was okay. When he saw that her door was open, he peeked in. His heart stopped. The room was empty, the bed neatly made. She wasn't in the bathroom. All her things were still in the closet and drawers.

Crazy thoughts rushed through his mind. Did she sleep-walk? Could she be outside? Had she taken his car and gone for a joyride? Was she so upset about her pregnancy that she might consider desperate measures?

It took him a full sixty seconds to get hold of himself. There had to be a plausible explanation.

He would search the house first. If that produced nothing in the way of answers, he might have to involve the police.

Fortunately for his galloping pulse, he found her almost immediately in the extra guest room. She was curled on her side in one of the narrow beds. Still on top of the covers, she was fully dressed except for her shoes that lay tumbled on the floor.

He leaned against the wall, breathing harshly. The kind of fear that had swept through him wasn't logical. But then again, none of his reactions to Cassidy Corelli fell into the realm of rationality.

The depth of his anxiety shocked him. In a very short time, she had done something to him…something unfathomable. She had made him want to love her.

But as much as he yearned to let go and wallow in the sunshine that was Cassidy Corelli, he was bound by his past. By the memory of getting burned. By the prospect of finding out that everything he thought he knew was a sham. What did it say about him that he couldn't take her bubbly charm and artless innocence at face value?

Was he too cynical for such a woman?

When he regained a modicum of control, he picked her up gently. His heart clenched when her head lolled against his shoulder. In her bedroom, he tossed back the covers and deposited her gently on the mattress.

She roused despite his care. "Gavin?"

"You conked out in the other room." He brushed the hair from her forehead. Her cheeks were flushed, her gaze heavy with sleep. "Close your eyes, Cass. It's late."

Her hand gripped his wrist. "Don't go."

The quiet entreaty undid him. Chances were she wouldn't have said it if she had been fully awake.

Chances were he could have refused it in broad daylight.

But the hour was late and his walls were down.

He leaned over her and found her lips. The taste still baffled him. Both exotic and sweet, the combination hit his weak spots. The need to pounce warred with the desire to cherish. She was so damned adorable.

The kiss lengthened, deepened. His mouth moved over hers lazily, as though they had all the time in the world. The room was quiet except for the sound of their breathing.

Her arms came up around his neck. "I want you, Gavin."

How could any man resist such a raw, honest statement? She asked for his unquestioning belief about her babies, and he couldn't give her that...not yet. But this he could offer. Pleasure. Connection. Two people meeting in the comforting dark and trying not to think about the struggles they faced outside these walls.

Deliberately, he reached out and turned off the bedside lamp.

Undressing was a dance, a slow, wistful ballet. First her clothes, then his. In the light from the hallway all he could make out was the shape of her. Any nuances of expression were lost in the shadows.

Probably just as well. He didn't want to see disappointment or regret in her beautiful eyes. She asked for faith and he had none. All he could give her was this.

Moving over and into her stopped time for a moment. He forced himself to release the breath he'd been holding. Strong, slender legs wrapped around his waist. "The babies?" he croaked.

He'd heard the doctor's assurances. Sex was fine. Sex was healthy for the mom and for the dad. But still he worried.

Cassidy cupped her hand behind his neck and pulled him down for a kiss. "They're good. I'm good. It's all good, Gavin."

Maybe it was and maybe it wasn't. Falling so deeply into the dream of having Cass forever wasn't good at all. He couldn't believe life happened in such a way. A chance meeting in an alley. A reckless night of sex and laughter. That was the stuff of movies.

Cassidy squeezed him with her inner muscles. "You're thinking," she complained. "Come back to me."

That she read him so well was also unsettling. Shutting

his brain to the endless sequences of events that could lead to disaster, he chose to live in the moment. She was warm and soft, so soft. Would he be able to take her like this in another four weeks? In eight?

Perhaps it would have to be from behind soon. That notion made him shudder. Tonight he had done his best to go slowly...to slide with purpose over the spot that ensured her pleasure.

But the madness beckoned now. His lungs strained for air. His loins ached. "Come with me, Cass," he pleaded.

She didn't answer, not verbally. But he heard her breath catch and felt her tremble against him.

Wildly, he thrust, chasing something just out of reach. She was his. He wanted it to be so. It *had* to be so. The fleeting thought that some faceless man might have fathered her babies made him insane.

He cried out her name when he came. The physical release was something more than pleasure, something less than peace. He felt incomplete and incoherent. Wanting something so badly and knowing he was the only obstacle in the way.

Cass's hands petted him, smoothed his shoulders, glided over his back. "Sleep with me," she cajoled.

It was the easiest request she'd ever asked of him.

"Yes," he muttered. He was loath to separate his body from hers.

In the end, he simply rolled to one side and dragged her against him before covering them both with the quilt.

Cassidy yawned. "Did you have any luck with the computer stuff?"

She was relaxed and warm and on the verge of sleep. "We'll talk about it in the morning," he said.

"Okay...good night, Gavin."

I love you, Cass...

Thirteen

Gavin awoke sometime later to the realization that Cassidy was climbing out of bed. "Where are you going?" he mumbled, not happy about losing his bedmate.

"I have to pee," she whispered.

He grinned in the dark. Being a woman was no easy task. But then he sobered. Cass would need someone at her side to care for her in the months ahead. She was strong and self-sufficient, but pregnancy was hard, especially with twins. He would keep her here as long as she would stay.

His present circumstance pointed out the flaw in his plan. He'd said *no more sex*...and yet here he was. A little voice inside his head posited the notion that Cassidy might be trying to lull him into complacence. That perhaps she thought by appealing to his masculine hungers she could win him over and make him believe what she wanted him to believe.

When she returned to the bed, her feet were cold. He rubbed them with both of his, shoving aside the thoughts that troubled him. He couldn't hold her without wanting her. His sex rose strong and eager.

"Cass?"

"Hmm?"

"You feel up to round two?"

She reached between them and gave him a naughty squeeze. "I could be persuaded…"

As Gavin eased her thighs apart and caressed her before entering her, Cassidy blinked back tears, hating the ready emotions that ambushed her without warning. Growing up, she'd never been a girlie girl when it came to feelings. Her dad had been very fair in that way. He expected Cassidy *and* Carlo to *suck it up*.

Scraped knees, disappointments with school friends, anything that could upset a kid…Gianni Corelli insisted his children put on a brave face. Cassidy had received no exemption for being a girl.

These past few weeks, she barely knew herself. Laughter turned easily to tears and vice versa.

The hardest thing right now was not letting Gavin see how emotional she was about their lovemaking. Being intimate with him made her soar with happiness. But in the aftermath, her doubts and worries returned full force.

He brushed his thumb across her cheek, finding dampness. "What's wrong, Cass?"

Inside her, he flexed and thickened, their connected bodies a precious reminder of her pregnancy. "Not a thing. Don't mind me. I've never been pregnant before. These mood swings take some getting used to."

"You could have said no."

"I didn't want to say no. I wanted you."

"It's tough on a guy's ego when the woman cries."

"Haven't you heard of happy tears?"

"Is that what these are?" He caught one with his fingertip. "Are you happy right now?"

She swallowed hard. *Was* she happy? She was making love to the only man she'd ever been with, the man who had—with her—created two miracles. Two new lives. She should be over the moon. But life wasn't that simple. Not when she knew Gavin wasn't prepared to take her word about the paternity of her children. His children.

Even knowing the reasons behind his inability to trust, it hurt.

She swallowed her reservations and her disappointment. *Suck it up.* "I'm happy," she said, only half lying. "I already love these babies, and I'm happy to be here with you."

He didn't answer. At least not verbally. But he rolled to his back and took her with him, settling her astride his hips. "Cry if you have to, Cass, as long as they're happy tears."

She wasn't able to climax this time. And she was pretty sure he realized it. Exhaustion and worry and a brand-new her combined to rob her of the response she wanted to give.

As he went rigid and choked out her name, his hands bruising her hips, she leaned forward and kissed him, feeling the trembling he couldn't hide. Maybe Gavin didn't trust her. Maybe he didn't love her. And maybe he didn't want to be a dad.

But one thing was clear. He wanted her. Every bit as much as she wanted him.

Morning found her once again hunched over the kitchen sink. Only this time Gavin accompanied her from the bedroom. In fact, as soon as he realized she was in distress, he scooped her up and carried her down the hall, both of them naked as the day they were born.

When he fetched saltines and plain tea and put them at her elbow, he kissed her nape. "Will you be okay if I go get your robe?"

She nodded, her breathing shallow as she willed away the nausea. But this time she lost the battle. While he was gone, she emptied her stomach. When he returned, she had just finished cleaning up the sink. Weak and weary, she let him tuck her into the robe and tie the sash.

"I need to sit down," she muttered. At least she wouldn't have to worry about gaining too much weight if this trend kept up.

Gavin had donned a robe that matched hers. He brought her untouched tea and crackers to the table. "Try to eat something, Cass. You'll feel better."

"My head knows that, but my stomach keeps voting *hell, no*."

Gavin chuckled quietly. But he was smart enough to let her be miserable in peace as she nibbled and sipped. It was a full half hour before she could actually swallow without any fear of gagging.

By that time, the sun was all the way up and Gavin's cozy kitchen was filled with warm, beautiful light.

He leaned his chair back on two legs and studied her face. "Your color is better. More death-warmed-over than zombie corpse."

"You do know how to flatter a girl."

"Should I tell you how nicely that robe shows off your cleavage?"

She glanced down, mortified. The lapels gaped, exposing her chest almost to the navel. "Why didn't you say something?"

His quick grin was full of masculine appreciation. "I was enjoying the view."

Slowly, she stood up, gratified that the room spun for only a couple of seconds. "I think I'll go take a shower."

Gavin touched her hand. "I have something to tell you about the casino. It's not good. Do you want to hear it right off or when you've had a chance to get dressed and your stomach quits doing acrobatics?"

She stared at him. Now the queasy feeling in the pit of her belly had nothing to do with pregnancy. "How bad?"

"Bad enough." His expression was sober.

Sinking back into her chair, she braced herself mentally. "I've always believed in ripping off the Band-Aid as quickly as possible. Don't keep me in suspense. What did you find out?"

"It took longer than I expected. You'll be glad to know that the casino's online security is actually damned impressive. I had to dig pretty deep to find answers."

"You're stalling."

He shrugged. "It's your brother."

She gaped at him. "Carlo?"

"Do you have another brother?"

The news was too incredible for her to quibble over his sarcasm. "But why?"

"I haven't a clue. Your father was on target about the amount. From what I could tell, the money has been moved ten to twenty thousand dollars at a time to three separate offshore accounts."

"I can't believe it." She *knew* Carlo. He might not have her work ethic, but he wasn't a criminal.

"The only other explanation is that he might have inadvertently given someone access by sharing his passwords and usernames."

"He wouldn't have done that. My father taught us from the time we were in high school to keep that stuff absolutely private." Yet she had shared hers with Gavin. She had infinite trust in him.

"Well, then, I think we've found the source of the theft. How do you want to handle this?"

A shiver ran down her spine as she imagined her father's reaction to the news that his beloved son was stealing. "I'll have to tell Daddy in person. This is not the kind of thing you can do over the phone."

"We, the Kavanaghs I mean, have a small jet that we share with a couple of other businesses. It's parked on an airstrip outside of town. My brother Patrick is a licensed pilot if you're game. It would be quicker than flying commercial out of Asheville, and more comfortable than first class."

"You own a jet?" Even Gianni Corelli wasn't that much of a high roller.

"We *share* a jet," Gavin said.

"Same difference," she muttered. She had barely adjusted to the change in time zones and now already she was going to head back across the country. The idea made her tired just thinking about it. But there was no point in delaying. Especially if money was continuing to disappear.

"How soon can we leave?" she asked.

"I'll contact Patrick. Depending on his schedule and if the jet's not already spoken for, we could fly out this afternoon."

"Make the call," she said, her stomach in a knot.

Gavin leaned across the table and squeezed her hand. "I won't let your father badger you or upset you. It's not good for you *or* the babies."

His gentle kindness in the midst of everything that was going on made her want to throw herself into his arms. Instead, she summoned a smile. "Thank you, Gavin. I appreciate your help."

Gavin did his best to keep an eye on Cassidy without her catching on that he was hovering. She sat in her wide comfy seat with her legs curled beneath her. They had both dressed for the upcoming meeting with her dad. Cass wore a scoop-necked, short-sleeved ivory angora sweater with black dress pants and chunky coral jewelry. With her hair pulled back in a loose ponytail, she looked young and beautiful.

He'd seen the look in his brother's eyes when he introduced Cassidy to Patrick. It was a masculine reaction that couldn't be masked. Cass made an impression.

She'd been charming and friendly before Patrick took the pilot's seat. Now her gaze was glued to the small window as they soared across the miles. He had a feeling she wasn't really seeing anything in particular. She was pale and subdued.

Her profile made him ache. So feminine, so sweet. But not weak. Far from it. She was smart and focused, despite the recent upheaval in her life. Once this business with her father and brother was settled, Gavin had a decision to make.

He knew in his gut that Cassidy's babies were his. And he knew there was no conspiracy. Or at least he was almost sure. Making love to Cassidy last night had stripped everything down to life's most basic level. She wasn't a liar or a cheat. He'd known that all along, though he hadn't been willing to admit it. Now life had dropped something wonderful in his lap. Something he hadn't asked for… something he hadn't expected.

Maybe sometimes, *knowing* someone had nothing to do with the calendar and everything to do with recognizing a person's character. If he followed up on his one wild night in Vegas…if he gave himself over completely to the idea that he and Cass were soul mates, his whole life would change.

Was he willing to place his trust in such an ephemeral dream?

Quietly, he unfastened his seat belt and crouched in the

aisle beside her seat. "Hey," he said quietly. "You feeling okay?"

She had her arms clasped around her waist in a protective posture. She nodded slowly. "I'm fine."

"I'm not so sure you are."

"Since when is the oh-so-practical Gavin Kavanagh a mind reader?"

"I'm beginning to figure out how *yours* works."

Finally, he coaxed a smile from her. "It's dangerous for a man to think he understands women," she said.

"Is that so?"

She patted his arm. "We are mysterious creatures."

"Like unicorns?"

"Don't make fun of me. Besides, there's a difference between mythical and mysterious. I'm very real."

Their gazes clashed, hers mischievous, his rueful. "It's taken me a little while to accept that. Everything about that night in Vegas seemed like a dream."

"For me, too, Gavin. I am a pretty responsible person most of the time. So I can't really explain what happened except to say that you were so terribly earnest and sweet when you rescued me."

"I'm not sweet," he growled, insulted by her description. "I did what any man would do."

"My brother is big and brawny and three inches taller than you. But even though you thought he was some kind of thug, you rushed in and did battle for my honor."

"Somebody's been reading too many romance novels."

"Don't disparage an entire genre. Whether you like it or not, you acted like a hero."

He shook his head, wishing he hadn't gone down this particular path. Which meant that changing the subject was in order. "Have you planned out what you're going to say to your dad?"

She rubbed her temples, the line of her mouth grim. "I'd like to say yes, but the truth is, I'm dreading it. The last time I saw him, he was yelling and throwing me out of his house."

"Would you like me to be there with you when you talk to him?"

Shock colored her face. "In what capacity?"

He knew what she wanted him to say. But he couldn't do it. Not quite yet. Maybe he had it in him to face down a bully, but this thing with Cassidy was another story. "As a friend," he said. "For now."

Seeing her disappointment at his answer made his stomach hurt. She called him a hero, but the truth was, he was afraid. Afraid to find out that he was being used…that he was blind to her faults…that she'd lied about who she was.

Only moments before, she had laughed and teased him, despite her anxiety about this trip to Vegas. Now, thanks to him, she had closed herself behind a veil of indifference.

"Yes," she said. The single word flat. "That would be helpful." She deliberately turned her face away from him, shutting him out.

But he deserved it.

When they landed in Vegas, Patrick stayed behind to take care of the formalities. Gavin had ordered a car to pick them up. It whisked them in short order to Cassidy's father's casino.

Gavin paid the fare and took Cass's arm. "How do we do this?"

She stood on the street, staring up at the building as if she had never seen it before. "I sent a text to my father's secretary. He's in his office. We'll go up and get it over with."

With his hand at her back, he followed her through the crowds to a private elevator at the back of the building. As the small cube whisked them upward, he leaned against the wall and studied his companion. Was it his imagination, or could he see a small baby bump?

The thought made his heart race. Imagining Cassidy rounded and glowing in the advanced stages of pregnancy was a kick to the gut...in a good way.

"Cass," he said impulsively.

She lifted her chin. She had been studying her shoes intently. "Yes?"

"When we get back to Silver Glen, you and I need to settle some things." He was trying to tell her that he was on board...that he was ready to accept fatherhood. But she took it the wrong way.

What little color there was in her cheeks faded. He saw her throat work as she swallowed. "You're right," she said quietly. "But let me get through this first."

He tried to answer, to correct whatever misconceptions she had, but the doors to the elevator opened, and the moment was lost. As they made their way down a long hall, he was impressed by the elegant Oriental runner and the silken wallpaper. Even in areas of the casino closed to the public, no expense had been spared.

Gavin put a finger beneath his collar and tugged. He'd worn a suit and tie as befitted his role in this upcoming drama, but he was tense and uneasy. Not for himself, but for Cassidy.

Though she had glossed over it when she came to North Carolina, he knew she had been deeply hurt by her father's reaction to her pregnancy. Cassidy was determined to be the one to break the news about who was stealing the money. But if her dad was verbally abusive to her in any way, Gavin would intervene.

He was not about to let anyone make Cassidy feel bad about herself. Or to be insulted or belittled.

He stood by her side as she knocked. Turning the knob, she opened the door and they both stepped inside. "Hello, Daddy," she said. "I need to talk to you."

Fourteen

Cassidy could feel Gavin at her back, his warm, solid presence a silent comfort. Perhaps she should have done this on her own. Perhaps it was cowardice to need backup. But she couldn't be sorry he had come with her. It was the only thing propelling her forward at the moment.

Gianni Corelli rose to his feet slowly, his gaze darting from his daughter to Gavin and back again. His bushy eyebrows drew together. "Is this the scoundrel who—"

Cassidy cut him off with a chopping motion of her hand. She wouldn't lie outright to her father, but today was not the time to dissect her untimely pregnancy. There were more urgent matters at hand.

She touched Gavin's arm briefly, feeling the strength of muscles beneath his jacket sleeve. In dress clothes, it was readily apparent that he was a man from a privileged background. He was comfortable with wealth. But not owned by it.

"Daddy," she said, "this is Gavin Kavanagh, a friend of mine. His company deals with cyberattacks of all kinds. I asked him to dig into the money being stolen from you. He found the source of the theft."

Gianni Corelli sat down hard in his chair, his daughter's failings forgotten for the moment. He seemed older suddenly, almost frail, though he weighed almost two hundred and fifty pounds. "Tell me," he croaked.

Cassidy took a small chair and dragged it to the edge of the large desk. Sitting down quickly, she wondered if there was any easy way to do this. She took a deep breath, gazing at him with all the love she could muster. "It's Carlo, Daddy," she said, her heart aching for her parent.

Gianni frowned. "What do you mean, *it's Carlo*?"

"Carlo has been stealing money from the casino…from you. Don't ask me why, but it's true."

The old man stared at her aghast. His hands began to shake. She reached out and gripped both of them, trying to steady him. "Daddy…don't get upset. We'll get to the bottom of this."

He stared at her. "I love that boy. And he stabs me in the back?"

Cassidy had expected fury and outrage. But the reality was even worse. Her father was heartbroken. And perhaps for the first time in his life, at sea. His vigor and infuriatingly dictatorial personality changed in an instant. To Cassidy, it was astonishing. But the metamorphosis was clear proof of how much Gianni idolized Carlo.

Gavin appeared at her elbow. "Drink this, sir. It will help." He had poured a shot of whiskey from the decanter on the sideboard. Cassidy was so intent on her father she had almost forgotten Gavin's presence in the room. "Thank you," she whispered, brushing his hand with hers.

Gianni tilted his head and swallowed the amber liquid. When his chest rose and fell in a giant sigh, she knew they had turned a dangerous corner. He gathered himself visibly. After a moment of hushed silence on the part of everyone in the room, he leaned forward and pressed the button on his intercom. "Find my son. I need him in my office ASAP."

* * *

Cassidy looked to Gavin automatically for support. His encouraging smile helped calm her nerves. She knew he was worried about her. This stress couldn't be good for her or for the babies. Outwardly, she was calm and resolute, but inside, she was a mess.

The three of them were silent as the minutes ticked away on an antique mantel clock. Her father's fireplace was for show and far from necessary in Vegas, but he leaned toward the traditional when it came to decor, as in most other things in his life.

It was exactly twelve and a half minutes before Carlo knocked briefly at his father's door and entered. He stopped short when he saw his sister and Gavin.

"Cassidy," he said, his face lighting up. "I didn't know you were here. Is everything okay?"

Carlo's look of love and concern as he hugged her seemed genuine. She hugged him back. "I'm fine, Carlo. But Daddy needs to talk to you about something." She paused awkwardly, hoping the alley had been too dark the night Gavin punched Carlo for Carlo to recognize him. "And this is my friend Gavin." She waved a hand in Gavin's direction.

Gavin nodded, apparently content for the moment to stay out of the limelight. The two men were standing far enough apart to make shaking hands unnecessary. Carlo returned the nod and looked at his father. "What's up, Pop?"

Gianni rose to his feet, putting one hand on the back of his chair. "I know, Carlo." The three words were ice-cold. But Carlo didn't get it.

He frowned. "Know what?"

The genuine puzzlement on her brother's face made Cassidy wonder for one hopeful second if Gavin was mistaken. She stayed silent, waiting to see how her father would handle this dreadful moment.

Gianni scowled. "I know about the money."

Carlo tensed, his body language unmistakable. "I don't know what you mean." But there was no doubt in anyone's mind that he did. He paled beneath his golden tan, his expression hunted.

The older Corelli stepped out from behind his desk and walked toward his son, with Cassidy at his side. She wasn't sure what she could do, but she wanted to be close in case her father needed physical assistance.

To Carlo's credit, he didn't back up.

Gianni poked a finger in his son's chest. "You *stole* from me, boy. Don't you know that I would have given you anything you asked for?"

Carlo blanched, wild-eyed. "I can explain."

Cassidy inhaled sharply. "So you admit it?" Up until that moment, she had prayed there was some mistake, some confusion.

Her father shook his head, seeming to age before her eyes. "It makes no sense. You deliberately decimated your own inheritance? Or were you trying, perhaps, to make sure you received more than your share?"

Carlo was sweating now, though the room was cool. "I had a plan, Papa. Truly, I did. Let me tell you."

Cassidy's father folded his arms across his chest. "I fail to see how you deserve a hearing, given your appalling villainy, but let no one say that Gianni Corelli is not fair. Speak, boy."

"Can we sit down?" Carlo asked.

Cassidy breathed an inward sigh of relief when her father consented. The stress of this confrontation taxed her strength and threatened a return of the morning's queasiness.

The three of them settled into seats around the fireplace, Cassidy and her father on the sofa, Carlo in an adjacent armchair. Though she lifted an eyebrow and motioned for Gavin to join them, he gave a negative shake of his head.

Carlo leaned forward, elbows on his knees, head in his hands. "I wanted to make you proud of me," he muttered.

His father looked at him as if he were an alien species. "I do not think I have reached the age of senility," he said, shaking his head. "But you are speaking foolishness."

Cassidy felt a wave of sympathy for her younger brother. Growing up, he had been spoiled by their father. Though Carlo had always been a bit immature, this latest escapade took his peccadilloes to an alarming new level. "Carlo," she said softly. "Why don't you start from the beginning?"

At last he sat up straight, his broad shoulders filling out the dress shirt and expensive sport coat he wore. He was too handsome for his own good. Females everywhere swooned when faced with that sexy smile and dark-eyed gaze.

Cassidy understood that he had coasted through life up until this point on his looks and his charm. But if he were going to be her father's right-hand man, he sure as heck had better offer some kind of a decent explanation... and quickly.

"It was because of Cassidy," Carlo said quietly.

She blinked, shocked by the seeming attack.

Her father saved her from having to respond. He glared at his son. "I do not like the direction this is going."

"Hear me out, Papa." Carlo had regained his equilibrium, but was visibly troubled. "When you sent Cass away, I knew you were wrong to do so. But I didn't say anything, because I knew this was my chance to finally work by your side. All my life I've heard you say how smart Cass is and how ambitious…how much you admired her responsibility and her drive and her instincts for business."

Cassidy stared at her father. "You did?"

His sheepish nod astonished her. "Of course. You're my daughter. It made me proud that you were just like me."

Carlo shrugged, looking at his sister with resignation. "See? I could never live up to that. But suddenly, you blotted your copybook by getting pregnant…with no husband or father in sight. I had to do something quickly to solidify my spot as Corelli presumptive."

"But I was gone," Cass said. "The job was yours."

"Maybe, maybe not. But I knew if I could make Papa see me in a new light, I had an opportunity to impress him with my worth."

Gianni slammed a fist on his knee. "So you decided that defrauding your papa of half a million dollars was going to make me happy?" His voice rose to a shout at the end, renewing Cassidy's fears that her father's health might be at risk.

Carlo winced. "I knew you would be upset when you realized the money was missing. I was going to offer my help in finding the culprit. When I 'discovered' the stolen cash, my plan was to return it to you and reap the benefits of your gratitude. So help me God, that's the truth."

The room fell silent. Gavin wanted to believe the kid's story, though there was no real hard evidence to do so. But Carlo was seemingly transparent, his contrition real and touching. Though he wasn't all that much younger than Cassidy, he had a lot of growing up to do.

A man needed to pave his own way in the world, though certainly not at the expense of the innocent. Gavin found it in his heart to feel sorry for Carlo. But his most pressing concern was for Cassidy.

Her brother's actions had to be a slap in the face.

Gianni stared at his son, his expression inscrutable. "Who taught you how to do such a thing?"

"I fooled around with computer stuff in college. I'm good at it, Papa."

"Good enough to rob me blind." But the rejoinder held little heat. The old man looked at his daughter. "Do you believe him, Cassidy? You've always been good at reading people. Is Carlo telling me the truth?"

Gavin frowned, taking an instinctive step forward. Gianni was being cruelly unfair. Why should Cass be asked to implicate or exonerate her own brother?

Cassidy stood up, her expression hard to read. "Excuse me, please." She made a beeline for the private bathroom that occupied a large corner of Gianni's office.

Neither Gianni nor Carlo seemed perturbed by her abrupt departure. Gianni shook his head. "I want the money back in the casino accounts by tomorrow morning at eight. Are we clear?"

Carlo nodded. "Yes, sir. Does that mean you believe me?"

Gianni scowled. "I need time to think about it. I will consult with your sister and let you know."

It was the most painful thing he could have said. Carlo slumped in his chair, defeat in every line of his posture. It had become very clear to Gavin in the past half hour that Gianni's brand of parenting was manipulative at best. He had pitted his children against each other, and sadly, the consequences were emotional bloodshed.

Cassidy's tenure in the bathroom was longer than Gavin would have liked. His radar was already on high alert when she finally emerged. In an instant he knew there was trouble.

"Cass," he said urgently, going to her and putting an

arm around her waist despite the eyes watching. "What's wrong?"

She leaned into him, hands clinging to his forearms, her brown eyes wide with panic. "I'm bleeding," she said. "Oh, Gavin, I'm bleeding."

In an instant all thoughts of the stolen money or Carlo's perfidy were forgotten. Cassidy's brother had his cell phone in his hand. "I'll dial 911."

Gianni shook his head vehemently. "It will take too long with traffic." He pointed at Gavin. "You, boy. Take her yourself. The closest hospital is only three blocks away. I'll have a car meet you downstairs at the back door service entrance. Carlo and I will be right behind you."

Gavin scooped Cassidy into his arms. She didn't protest. That scared him most of all. "I'll take care of her," he said, giving the two Corelli males one last glance. The two men, so much alike in build and coloring, had identical expressions on their faces. Fear.

It was a good bet that Gavin's face looked exactly the same.

Reversing the route he and Cass had followed to access her father's office seemed to take forever. He held her tightly, as if he could literally keep her safe. But today's danger was not something as clear-cut as a bully in an alley. It was internal…potentially devastating.

In the elevator, he looked down at his precious cargo. She was crying. "Ah, God. Don't, Cass. I can't bear it. Everything is going to be okay."

"You keep saying that," she whispered, "but it seems to be getting worse. This is my fault," she said.

"No." He didn't know how to comfort her.

"Yes. It's true. In the very beginning I didn't want this pregnancy. Now I'm being punished."

"The world doesn't work that way. Neither does God

or fate or any other force of nature. Not every woman is ecstatic when she finds out she's pregnant. But would you give those babies up now if you could?"

"Of course not."

"Then hush, sweetheart. Don't upset yourself more. This has been a hell of a day."

With Cassidy's help, he located the door to the delivery bay. As promised, a car was waiting. Gavin tucked Cass into the backseat and ran around to the other side of the car to join her. Only then did he realize this was the spot where he had first met her.

At another day and time, he might have paused to smile at the irony. But now was not the moment for reflection. He leaned toward the driver. "To the hospital. And hurry."

The medical facility was modest in size, but completely modern and fully equipped. Everything worked like a well-oiled machine. The wait time in emergency was only fifteen minutes, which seemed like a miracle to Gavin. He was prepared to do battle, but when they took Cassidy back, he followed and no one protested.

The nurse, however, did oust him while she helped Cassidy into a gown and checked her stats. When he was allowed to return, the woman in scrubs gave him a smile. "The doctor will be in very shortly. Hopefully ten or fifteen minutes. You picked a good time to come. It's been pretty quiet here today." She exited the room moments later.

Cassidy looked pale and small in the hospital gown. "Hold my hand," she said, stretching out her arm.

He gripped her fingers with his, trying to telegraph courage. She didn't speak, and he didn't know what to say to her. Finally, when the burden of silence became too great to bear, he sighed. "Are you hurting?"

"No."

"Is there much…uh…"

"Not a lot…but not a little."

"Is it because we had sex last night?" The possibility tormented him.

"I don't know. Miscarriage is fairly common in the early weeks."

"You're not having a miscarriage," he said firmly. "Don't think that way."

Finally, the doctor came in. Although it had seemed like a long wait, when Gavin glanced at his watch, he saw that the nurse's estimate had been spot-on.

The emergency room physician looked barely old enough to be out of med school. But he seemed confident and knowledgeable. "Let's see what's going on," he said as he pulled out the stirrups.

Cassidy glanced up at Gavin. "Would you step outside, please?" She tried to pull her hand free.

He tightened his grasp instinctively. "But I…"

The doctor nodded, though his gaze was kind. "We won't be long."

Gavin had no choice but to cooperate. He went into the hall and shut the door. In the old days, emergency rooms had curtains. But now that privacy laws were so stringent, even these cubicles had standard doors.

What was happening inside? Why had Cassidy asked him to leave?

It seemed like eons before he was summoned. The doctor poked his head out the door. "You can come back in now."

When Gavin returned to the small room, he found Cassidy sitting up on the end of the exam table and the doctor washing his hands. The man spoke over his shoulder. "Everything looks perfectly fine. It's not uncommon for fluctuating hormone levels at this stage to prompt some bleeding. She'll be fine. It wouldn't hurt to rest tomorrow, but after that, resume activity as normal."

Gavin cleared his throat. "So it was nothing we did?"

The doctor's smile was professional but sympathetic. "Not at all. Ms. Corelli said she's been under a lot of stress…and I understand she flew cross-country today. But to be honest, I would seriously doubt that this was anything other than an isolated incident. We'll do some blood work to make sure. I don't think we have any reason to admit her, though."

When the man in the lab coat exited, Gavin wanted to talk to Cassidy. But before he could do so, Gianni and Carlo arrived. Cassidy's father leaned down to kiss her. "What's happening? Are you okay?"

Cassidy nodded. "The doctor says so. He thinks it's a hormonal thing and very normal."

"Thank God." Gianni touched her hand, his smile tentative. "I owe you an apology, my daughter. I reacted poorly when you told me you were pregnant. I want you to come home. You and Carlo will *both* work by my side. I take some of the responsibility for his foolishness. I thought it was a good thing for the two of you to compete, but I see now that I was wrong."

Cassidy stared at her father. "But you believe that women should stay home and raise children."

Gianni shrugged. "I am old-fashioned, what can I say? If you want to be a mother to your children and still work at the casino, I will try to adjust. I don't want to lose you, Cassidy. You are my dear daughter, and I see your mother in you every day. Besides, practically speaking I need your instincts and training to help me keep up with the times."

"This is a big turnaround for you."

"Yes. But today I saw what my stubborn ways drove

my son to attempt. I would hate for you to do anything so foolish. We are a family, we three Corellis. We belong together."

Carlo spoke not a word during all of this. Finally, Gavin saw Cassidy stare at her brother. "Say something, Carlo."

His smile was rueful. "I want you to come home, too. And I'm sorry for being such an idiot."

Cassidy shook her head. "The funny thing is, I was always jealous of *you*, Carlo. If we actually try to work together instead of against each other, imagine all we can accomplish."

Gianni nodded. "We will get out of here now. Give us a call when you're ready to come home."

Fifteen

Cassidy reeled. A huge portion of her life had done a one-eighty turn. Instead of being the disgraced child, Cassidy had heard a retraction with her own ears. Her father actually said he needed her. Perhaps if she looked out the window, she would see pigs fly.

Only Gavin remained a problem. And sadly, this relationship was not going to be tied up so neatly in a bow. The exam room was tiny. Four adults had occupied the space, and yet not once had her father acknowledged Gavin's presence.

Surely he wondered why the cyber expert who tracked down Carlo's culpability was hanging around in the midst of a pregnancy scare. Anyone with half a brain could figure out that Gavin and Cassidy had some kind of relationship.

But Gianni Corelli, for once, hadn't butted in. Perhaps it was his silent way of finally acknowledging that Cassidy was a grown woman and capable of making her own decisions.

She took a deep breath. "Would you mind stepping outside again so I can get dressed?"

Gavin straightened from where he had been leaning against the wall. "I've seen you naked."

The statement was flat…uninflected. But it made her flush nevertheless. "This is different."

She held his gaze with difficulty. Finally, he nodded. But on his terms. "I'll turn my back, Cass. That's all you're getting."

Dressing hurriedly was an act of cowardice. She couldn't bear the thought of being vulnerable in front of him. There were things to be done, and she needed whatever armor she could find.

When she was decent, she muttered, "Okay."

Gavin faced her, his hands in his pockets. "That's it? Carlo is forgiven? I thought you said your father would be upset."

"He was. He is. But everyone makes mistakes, Gavin. Carlo is family. He did a stupid thing, but Daddy won't kick him out."

"He kicked *you* out."

"Yes." She sighed. "But he apologized. I don't want to spend my life being mad at him. He's my children's grandfather."

"So what now?"

With a tiny prayer to the patron saint of acting, if there was such a thing, she smiled normally. "You and Patrick go home. I appreciate all you've done. When the babies are born, I'll contact you and we can arrange for a paternity test if you are still interested. After that you can make a decision about how much or how little involvement you would like to have."

His eyes narrowed. "So pragmatic. Problem solved. You're really going to ignore the fact that we have this insane chemistry between us?"

What did he want from her? Was she supposed to blurt out her love when he had been nothing but suspicious of her from the beginning? She might be brave, but she wasn't that brave.

"Of course I care about you, Gavin," she said calmly as

her heart was breaking. "But I have my life to lead and you have yours." She couldn't stay with him for the twins… not without something beyond sexual attraction. It would destroy her. She needed more than a father for her babies. She needed Gavin's love and trust.

"So that's it? You're staying here?"

"You heard Daddy. Everything is forgiven. I appreciate your taking me in when I came to North Carolina, but thankfully your house can get back to normal. If you would ship my things to me, I would appreciate it."

Now ice replaced the heat. "God, you're a piece of work. You never would have sought me out if it weren't for the pregnancy, would you?"

"I'm not the one who left Vegas and never looked back."

Where had it sprung from? Such bitter enmity? The memory of their first night together in this very town was so sweet and wonderful. Yet they had come to this.

She wanted him to say he loved her…to beg her to marry him…to demand that she return to North Carolina and claim her rightful place as the mother of his children.

But Gavin did none of those things. He simply stared at her with hot eyes, eyes that judged her and found her wanting.

At last when she couldn't bear the standoff one second longer, he put his hand on the door. "Have a nice life, Cassidy."

The angry sarcasm flicked her on the raw. "Don't forget to send me a bill for the jet trip. I'm a Corelli. We can afford it."

Whatever bleak expression she saw in his gaze must have been mirrored on her face. She couldn't believe she had been so nasty to him. Maybe they were not good for each other at all. Perhaps if they stayed together, his cynicism would drag her down.

He shook his head as if trying to free himself from a bad dream. "It's on the house," he said, the tone glacial. "Consider it payment for our one wild night in Vegas."

Gavin walked the streets of the neon city for an hour before he was calm enough to go in search of his brother. He found Patrick at Mandalay Bay feeding quarters into a slot machine.

Patrick looked up in surprise. "Where's Cassidy?"

Gavin couldn't quite meet his little brother's gaze. He was still raw inside. "She's with her family. Where she belongs. If you're up to it, I'm ready to fly home."

Patrick's face fell. "I thought we were staying a couple of days."

"Maybe another time." Maybe when hell froze over. He never wanted to set foot in Vegas again. Cassidy had given him the ephemeral promise of happiness and warmth, but it was all a sham. He'd made another mistake with a woman. And this time, he might never recover.

Cassidy found healing in work and in the steady, burgeoning presence of her twins. She talked to them constantly. Every night before bed she read them stories.

Her relationships with her father and her brother improved daily. Carlo's faux pas had given him a dose of humility. And Gianni Corelli was trying to change his attitude about women. Both men had Italian blood in their veins…and centuries of chauvinistic history. But even so, they were making an effort, and Cassidy appreciated it.

In the dark of the night when there was no work to do and no stories to be read, she thought about Gavin. She told herself the pain would get better…that she wouldn't crave his touch every second of the day. But in that arena, she hadn't made much progress. No crying, though. It wasn't good for the babies. Cassidy would be strong for them. She and her twins would build a family together.

Whenever she thought about the future, it was in terms of how she would manage to be mother and father at the same time. She'd waited her whole life for a man to come along who would be her perfect ideal of a mate. Someone strong and caring and decent and kind.

Maybe that was asking too much. Maybe that was her problem. It wasn't really fair to ask Gavin to be an instant father. Not when the only contact he'd had with her was that one night in Vegas.

Admittedly, since then he had shown a marked interest in taking her to bed, but sexual attraction wasn't strong enough glue to hold a relationship together when neither of the parties really knew each other. That wasn't quite true, though. She *did* know Gavin, maybe more than he realized. She had seen his relationship with his mother and his brothers. She'd witnessed his attempt to help her and shelter her even in the midst of his doubts.

There were so many reasons she had fallen in love with him. But she made the choice to cherish the memories and not be sad. Gavin needed someone in his life. She was convinced of that. But clearly, it wasn't her.

She thought about moving out of her father's house and getting her own place. She would need help after the birth, though, so that wasn't really practical. Her father wouldn't be much assistance, but Carlo was actually getting excited about the twins.

The day the beautiful baby furniture arrived unexpectedly from North Carolina, Cassidy broke her no-crying rule. After Carlo helped her assemble the crib, he took off to play basketball with some friends. Gianni was at the casino. Cassidy sat in the middle of the floor in the babies' room and sobbed.

The day she and Gavin had picked out those pieces, she really hoped everything was going to be okay. She'd even begun to imagine how she might use her training and talents to start some kind of business in Silver Glen.

But she'd been both misguided and naive.

Twice now she'd thought about flying to Silver Glen to see if there was any kind of chance with Gavin. But twice she talked herself out of it. If he wanted her, he would have come. His silence spoke volumes.

The day arrived when she had to put away her stylish clothes and don maternity tops and pants. She wore them proudly, not at all worried about gaining too much weight. Heartbreak had a way of keeping the pounds in check.

Still, it took her by surprise when she walked past a mirror and saw her rounded belly. Being pregnant was both magical and exhausting. The morning sickness had finally abated, but the fatigue remained.

She found herself counting the days until her due date, in part because she was excited, but also because once the twins were born, she would have an excuse to contact Gavin.

What would he say when that day came? Would he even consent to a paternity test? The man was an enigma...

Gavin acquired three new clients in the weeks following his return from Vegas...big clients. He stayed busier than ever, troubleshooting problems and making suggestions for improvement to the businesses in his care.

The thing with Cassidy felt uncomfortably like failure. And failure was rarely part of his vocabulary. He had been almost ready to confess to Cassidy that he believed her about the babies and that he wanted her to stay...maybe forever. But then her father had taken her back with open arms and Gavin had lost his bargaining chip.

If Gavin thought there was a chance she could fall in love with him, he would have said something. But he'd trapped her with an unintended pregnancy. She was young and bright and beautifully alive, and she deserved a man better than he was, a man who hadn't spent far too many years bound by his cynicism. He told himself things ended as they should have. But deep down, he didn't believe it, particularly in the middle of the night when he was aching and sleepless.

Cassidy had brightened up an existence he hadn't even recognized as gray. She'd made him want…had made him feel.

He was accustomed to keeping his own counsel, but the situation ate away at him. He should talk to somebody. Anybody. But his pride got in the way.

So he couldn't decide if it was a good thing or a bad thing when Conor showed up one afternoon. Gavin had just changed into running clothes and was sitting on the back porch tying his shoes. His brother was attired similarly. Gavin eyed him with suspicion. "This is a little coincidental, don't you think?"

Behind Gavin's house, a three-quarter-mile trail led up the side of the mountain. The route was steep and rocky and challenging. His custom was to run up and back three times.

Conor grinned and shrugged. "You're a creature of habit. And I could use the exercise. Race you to the top."

Before Gavin could stand up, Conor took off, his long legs eating up the distance. Gavin's competitive instinct kicked in. No way in heck was he going to let his baby brother beat him.

Conor, however, was a skier and a natural athlete. Gavin was determined, but Conor had a head start. They made it to the top and turned around, hurtling downward on the narrow trail at breakneck speeds. At the bottom, they started all over again.

At the start of the fifth trip to the top, Gavin began to question his sanity. Sweat poured down his back and dripped into his eyes. His thigh muscles screamed. His lungs burned.

Conor's pace had slowed noticeably, but so had Gavin's. They changed position frequently, either elbowing each other out of the way or sliding past if the other one paused to breathe.

At the completion of five circuits, Conor held up his hand. "Enough." He leaned forward, both hands on his knees, his labored gasps audible.

Gavin joined him, mimicking his stance. "What was that about?" he asked.

"You've been hiding out. It's not good for the soul."

"Since when did you become a philosopher?"

Conor didn't bother to answer the rhetorical question. He straightened and swiped his arm over his forehead. "Humidity's a bitch today."

Gavin agreed, but that was hardly the point. "Why are you here, Conor?"

Conor's eyes danced with mischief, despite his fatigue. "Patrick told me he met your sexy visitor. Said he took the two of you to Vegas."

"Patrick should mind his own damned business."

"He told me Cassidy is a sweetheart."

Gavin felt his neck tighten. "Patrick can stay the hell away from Cassidy."

"Why? You don't want her."

Gavin saw red. Literally. His response was gut-deep and fierce. He swung his fist at Conor's jaw and connected with a satisfying crack that sent pain shooting down his arm. Conor staggered backward, but remained standing.

His younger brother rubbed his chin, his expression no longer lighthearted. "You are one screwed-up sonofabitch."

Gavin agreed with him, but a man never showed weakness. "I'm doing just fine."

"Listen to me, Gavin. I know you. You're a perfectionist. You never allow yourself to make a mistake because of what happened when you were twenty-one."

"You mean when I was a credulous fool and ended up in jail?" Even now the memory was raw, though buried deep.

Conor leaned against a support beam for the porch. "Maybe I never told you, but Patrick and I admired the hell out of you back then. Still do for that matter."

"I don't want to talk about this."

"You went to *jail*, Gavin. For five long nights. Because you knew you were innocent and you wouldn't let your own family bail you out. It wasn't your fault the woman you met was psycho. It was your first date. You paid for it with a hell of a big tab. From where I'm standing, you're still paying."

It pissed Gavin to hear his little brother lay out the truth so neatly and with such painful accuracy. "I should have known," he muttered.

"*Any* guy would have done the same. She was cute and sexy and she came on to you. How were you supposed to anticipate that she would cry rape?"

"Did you know Mom wanted to pay the hush money?"

"Not because she thought you were guilty."

"Then why?"

"She couldn't bear the thought of your being in jail. None of us could."

"You had doubts." It was the first time Gavin had ever said it out loud. The *only* time he had ever given voice to the stunning, sick feeling in the pit of his stomach.

Conor stared at him intently, as though trying to do

some Vulcan mind meld thing. "No. We were in shock and upset and worried. But we knew you weren't a rapist. God, Gavin. Give us some credit."

Gavin stared into the distance, unable to meet his brother's earnest gaze. The worst of what happened was in the past. His slate was wiped clean. What remained was the fear of being duped again.

"I barely know Cassidy."

Conor understood what he wasn't saying. "It's like being hit by a drunk driver, Gavin. The victim goes through all the what-ifs. But in the end, the accident is a quirk of timing. Sheer bad luck." He paused. "You did nothing wrong. You met a pretty woman on campus and asked her out on a date. She targeted you, but it didn't work. The likelihood of another such *accident* is less than nil. You've *been* with Cassidy, even if not for months and years. You know her. Trust your instincts. They won't steer you wrong. You're a mature man, not a kid anymore."

"Thank God." Gavin's muttered response was more of an honest prayer than Conor realized. "Thanks for the pep talk, little brother."

Conor rubbed the heel of his sneaker in the grass. "So what are you going to do?"

"About what?"

"Don't be dense. About Cassidy."

"I appreciate your concern, Conor. I really do. But I don't need help with my love life."

"Do you? Love her, I mean?"

There was no humor on Conor's face, no teasing, no sibling jostling for position. Only a deep compassion that made Gavin ache. His brother's empathy made him feel naked, stripped of all defenses.

Gavin swallowed hard. "How can I? If you add up the

time she and I have spent together, it wouldn't even equal a week."

"That's your excuse?"

"It's not an excuse, damn it. It's the truth."

Conor shook his head. "This is a worst-case scenario for you, isn't it? Love at first sight. Throwing caution to the wind. Poor Gavin. Maybe you should leave her alone after all. I'm not sure you can handle the fallout if you really are in love. Good luck, bro. You're gonna need it."

Sixteen

Gavin stood beneath the stinging spray of the shower and wrestled with his desires and his fears. Cassidy was a fun one-night stand. He had acted completely out of character that night. He needed time to decide what to do. But the clock was ticking, because Cassidy carried two small lives in her womb. Those babies wouldn't wait for Gavin to make a decision.

Conor's words had impacted Gavin. In a good way. But they didn't change the facts of the case. Cassidy wanted nothing more than to work by her father's side in the family business. She didn't need Gavin's money, because she had plenty of her own. Las Vegas and Silver Glen were miles apart in every way that counted.

So, the questions were pretty simple: *Did* Gavin love Cassidy? Did he trust her completely? Did he want to step out of the dark into a world of light and happiness? And was he willing to do whatever it required to make her his?

As she drove the short distance from the casino to the Corelli mansion, Cassidy thought about something Carlo had said recently. She'd been trying to convince him that she and her father had forgiven him. But Carlo had pointed out that it was much harder to forgive himself.

He was so right. Cassidy could forgive Gavin *his* doubts,

but she had a hard time excusing her own actions. She should have been completely honest and told Gavin that she had fallen in love with him. Maybe her admission would have made it easier for him to embrace his impending fatherhood and to admit he had feelings for her, as well. But maybe not.

She pulled into the garage and shut the door behind her. In the kitchen, she kicked off her sandals and poured herself a large glass of water. Drinking it slowly, she stood at the island and gazed around the room she had come to take for granted. She'd spent much of her time here over the years. Doing homework, playing cards with her brother, begging the housekeeper to teach her how to cook.

Now she was going to be a mother. But she had no guide to follow. Her own mom had died a long, long time ago.

She wanted more than anything for her babies to grow up knowing they were loved. Sharing custody was not ideal, but she hoped Gavin would be a real father. Someone for the children to lean on. And selfishly, she clung to the hope that one day Gavin might find it in his heart to trust her and forgive her and give her another chance.

She finished her drink and put the glass in the dishwasher. The sofa in the living room was comfortable, so she headed that way with the thought of taking a nap. But when she rounded the corner in the hall, she stopped dead. Gavin Kavanagh sat in one of the velvet-covered wingbacks, his hands behind his head, his legs outstretched in front of him.

Everything about his posture shouted relaxation.

"Gavin. You scared me to death."

"Carlo let me in. Sorry," he drawled. But he didn't look sorry at all.

His gaze zeroed in on her protruding stomach. Slowly, he rose to his feet. "My God. You're really pregnant."

The awe and wonder in his voice touched her. "Pretty sure you already knew that."

He shook his head. "That's not what I meant. *Really* as in *very*. Very pregnant." His hand hovered over her belly. "May I?"

"Of course." Most people didn't even ask. For whatever reason, pregnant women seemed to be fair game. But Gavin had helped create the little duo she carried.

Gavin settled his palm against the curve of her considerable baby bump. "Do you know yet about the sexes?"

His hand hadn't moved, but being so close to him was arousing. "No. Next week, I think."

At that exact moment, one of the twins kicked…hard.

Gavin jerked his hand away. The momentum nearly made him trip over an ottoman. "Was that one of the babies?"

She took his hand and put it back. "Yes. Be patient and you'll feel it again. It's amazing."

As she had promised, another large ripple briefly distended the surface of her belly.

Gavin's eyes met hers. "Incredible," he said hoarsely.

They were standing so close she could inhale the scent of him. His streaky brownish-blond hair was longer than when she last saw him. She touched the silky strands just above his ear. "You need a haircut."

"No time," he muttered. He took her hands in his. "Cassidy?"

"Yes?"

"I know the babies are mine."

Shock left her speechless.

He grimaced. "I've known it all along in my heart, but my head was slow to catch up. I'm sorry."

"I understood. It hurt. It *really* hurt, because you were the only man I'd ever trusted enough to be intimate with.

I understood, though, after talking with your mother, that I was paying for another woman's sins." His admission healed a tear in her heart, but it wasn't what she really wanted.

He shook his head. "That whole business when I was about to graduate from college…well…let's just say it shook me…made me doubt myself when it came to women."

"I can't imagine what you went through."

"The thing is, Cass…" When he stumbled to a halt, she frowned. She had never seen Gavin unsure of himself.

"What are you trying to say?"

He shrugged, his expression bleak. "I fell in love with you. I *am* in love with you. I know I hurt you by not trusting you about the babies, but I want you to know the truth. Even if you don't feel the same way."

She wanted to throw herself at him, but he looked more miserable than lovesick. "We both had some hurdles to face, Gavin. This situation has been tough for both of us."

"Spending five nights in jail was tough. But spending even five more minutes without you in my life will kill me. I love you, Cass. So damned much." He ran his thumb over her cheek. "My body recognized the truth that very first night. You were this perfect woman I had dreamed up, but you were real."

She had to blink to clear tears from her eyes. "Trust me, I'm not perfect."

"Perfect for me," he said, the words deep and firm. His gray eyes were clearer and more open than she had ever seen them.

"Oh, Gavin." She wrapped her arms around his neck, feeling a deep tide of gratitude wash over her. "I can't hug you like I want to," she complained. "I feel like a cow and I'm only five months along."

He kissed her softly, his lips lingering over hers until they both sighed. "It might be easier lying down."

She grinned. "Spoken like a man."

"Am I wrong?" He lifted an innocent eyebrow.

"Not at all."

Hand in hand, they walked down the hall to her bedroom. She wanted to shove him up against the nearest wall and demand that he ravage her, but this sweet reunion disarmed her completely.

With the door safely locked behind them, his hands went matter-of-factly to his shirt buttons. They undressed in silence as a huge lump of emotion clogged her throat. "I love you, too," she whispered. "Why else would I still be a virgin all this time if I hadn't been waiting for Mr. Right?"

He was nude now, his erection lifting against his abdomen. Freezing for one long second, he took a deep breath, staring meaningfully at her stomach. "Not exactly a virgin, Cass."

"You know what I mean." She wanted to cover herself with her hands, but as a full-fledged adult with a family on the way and the most amazing man in the world about to make love to her, she stood proudly in front of him.

Sweetness winnowed away, replaced by raw passion. The look in his eyes made her tremble.

He raked both hands through his hair, his expression agitated. "Is it okay? I don't want to hurt you…or them."

She went to him, resting her cheek against his chest, hearing the steady thump of his heart. "You won't. You can't. Be with me, Gavin. In all the ways there are. I want you so much."

He lifted her into his arms, not visibly strained by the fact that he carried not one but three individuals. Folding back the covers on her bed with one hand, he put her down gently and joined her.

"I won't ever walk away from you again." Reclining on his hip, he bent and kissed her belly. "You're beautiful inside and out, Cass. Funny and smart and full of life. We have things to discuss, but first things first."

He wouldn't move on top of her even though she coaxed. Instead, he spooned her. Lifting her leg over his, he entered from behind.

The position was interesting. But she soon lost any interest in Sex 101 when Gavin began to move inside her. The weeks of grief and stress melted away. Against all odds, she and Gavin were together again.

He held her firmly but gently, his body worshipping hers. The desultory pace began to make her frantic. Moving restlessly against him, she tried to get him to take the hint. "Please, Gavin. I'm so close."

He nipped the back of her neck with sharp teeth. "Don't rush me, woman. I've missed you. I want to savor the moment."

With his body surrounding her, she had no recourse but to close her eyes and reach for the tantalizing ripples of completion. When the end came, there was no doubt. She cried out, the whip of pleasure sharp and wicked. Already Gavin groaned and shuddered as they rode the wave together.

Gavin's heart thundered in his chest. His mouth was dry as cotton. But he held Cass's breast in his hand, so he didn't move, not even to disconnect their bodies. His head rested on her pillow, his thighs cradling hers.

When he thought he could speak, he muttered in her ear. "How do you feel?"

She yawned and stretched, turning on her back to look up at him. Her molten chocolate eyes glowed with happiness. "Shattered. Complete. Sexually sated. Giddy. Shall I go on?"

"Brat." He plucked at her nipple. The temptation to initiate round two was strong. But he had things to tell her.

When it looked as if she might fall asleep, he said her name. "Cassidy."

"Hmm?" She didn't even open her eyes.

"I know how important it is to you to work alongside your father and your brother. I'm prepared to move my entire business to Vegas so you can fulfill your dream."

Her eyes flew open. "You can't do that."

"Why not?"

"Because I won't let you. I don't want to take you away from your family and Silver Glen. I won't."

He could see that her indignation was genuine. The generosity it encompassed humbled him. "In that case," he said, "I have one other proposition to offer. What if we split our time between both states? And what if you join me as an equal partner in The Silver Eye?"

Any trace of drowsiness fled from her gaze. "Why?"

"I like the thought of working with you."

"I'm sorry, but the answer is no."

His heart fell to his knees. "Oh."

Cass shook her head with a rueful smile. "My whole life has been focused on the Corelli casino, in part because of competition with my brother. But the truth is, I've found other goals, other dreams. Carlo and I are in a good place now, and he's going to make my father and me proud."

"So what will you do?"

"That depends on you, I think."

He stared at her blankly. "How?"

"Did you perhaps intend to propose to me? But you forgot that part?"

He put a hand to his forehead, feeling the gradual return

of hope. "It's entirely possible," he said, his smile rueful. "Seeing you again scrambled my brain. Will you marry me, Cassidy Corelli, and have my babies?"

"Only if you understand that my being pregnant and in love with you is not a sacrifice. That I'm a grown woman making a decision about my future without coercion or regret."

"Then you're saying yes?"

"With pleasure, my sweet Gavin."

"There's one more thing," he said, stroking her rounded belly.

She rolled her eyes. "Sheesh. And they say women talk too much."

"Don't be a smart-ass when I'm being romantic."

"Sorry," she said, trying to look penitent and failing miserably. The happiness she felt was written all over her face.

Some of the sparkle even rubbed off on him. He ran his fingers across her brow, through her short, dark curls, his chest tight with emotion. There were so many ways he could have missed out on meeting her. If his friend hadn't gotten sick. If Gavin hadn't agreed to do the speech. If Gavin hadn't decided to take a walk around Vegas that night.

And now here he was...with Cass...having babies together. Making plans to get married. In love. It wasn't anything he'd anticipated, or anything he'd thought he wanted. But it was the best thing that had ever happened to him.

He tried not to let the sight of her soft, warm, curvy body sidetrack him. "What would you think about going to the wedding chapel and letting your cousin marry us? For real this time."

Cassidy's chin wobbled. "Seriously? I'd love it. But what about your family?"

"We can have a big fancy reception later…in Silver Glen. But today, I only want you, my love."

"Oh, Gavin…"

"Oh, Cassidy…" He mocked her teasingly, but he knew how she felt.

"There's only one thing."

His shoulders tensed. What now?

"Tell me," he said, bracing for the worst.

Long lashes fluttered in sync with a cajoling smile. "Can I please take a nap *before* we get married?"

Five hours later, Cassidy walked by Gavin's side as they approached Robbie's Elvis-themed wedding chapel. Gavin squeezed her hand. "Are you sure about this, sweetheart?"

She nodded, leaning her head against his shoulder. "Not a doubt in my mind." While she napped, Gavin had checked out marriage procedural details. With no waiting period and no blood tests, all they had to do was show up in person and procure the license.

After that, Gavin had spirited her away to an extremely posh maternity boutique to shop for a wedding gown. Despite trying on at least a dozen possibilities, in the end she had chosen a 1920s style dress in ivory pleated silk that left her shoulders bare except for narrow straps. The empire bodice was covered with bugle beads and antique crystals that caught the light when she moved.

A small fascinator concocted of lace and a single faux magnolia blossom perched on the side of her head, completing the look.

She looked in the trifold mirror, glancing over her shoulder to get the back view. "What do you think, Gavin?" She had pooh-poohed the idea that it might be bad luck for him to see her gown. She had been separated from him for several long weeks. Now she didn't want to let him out of her sight.

His eyes glittered with desire. "It's perfect...almost."

She frowned. "Almost?"

She stood on a six-inch-high circular platform. Gavin went down on one knee and drew a red leather box from his pocket. "I forgot to give you this."

This was a flawless solitaire set in a plain platinum band. The clarity and purity of the stone shot a thousand tiny rainbows across the room when he slipped the ring onto her left hand. "Now it's official," he murmured, kissing her knuckles.

When the door of the wedding chapel swung open, Cassidy snapped back to the present. Robbie's expression was priceless. "More games, Cass?" he asked with a baffled look.

She shook her head. "Nope." Handing over an envelope of cash, she smiled. "This is the real deal. Gavin and I want you to marry us."

Robbie glanced down at her very pregnant belly, revealed tastefully in ivory silk. "Left it a bit late, didn't you?"

She laughed. "Better late than never."

This time, although the setting was familiar, everything else seemed brand-new. Gavin's deep voice repeating vows. Robbie's much higher tenor stumbling only slightly as he spoke his parts of the ceremony.

When it was her turn, she wasn't nervous at all. *"To have and to hold, from this day forward..."* She spoke the words reverently, steadily, so very grateful that her family was going to be complete.

Through it all, Gavin stared at her with a look she never thought to see from the quiet, brooding Kavanagh male. It was one part fierce possession and one part pride.

Afterward, when the paperwork was signed and the formalities completed, Robbie got a funny look on his face.

Cassidy stared at him. "What is it? What's wrong?"

Sheepishly, her cousin reached under the counter and produced a bottle of very familiar-looking champagne. "I forgot the bubbly," he said. "And you actually paid for it this time."

Gavin plucked the green glass container out of his hand and kissed his bride. "Mrs. Kavanagh can't have alcohol at the moment, but we'll save it for when the babies are christened. Besides," he said, taking Cass's arm and walking her down the aisle, "it's gonna be one wild night in Vegas, with or without champagne."

Epilogue

Cass lay with her eyes closed, feeling as if her body was floating over the bed. She ached in every cell...in every hair follicle. But beneath the physical discomfort was a deep vein of peace.

The door opened quietly and a man's voice called. "Wake up, Mama. Your son and daughter are here."

When she opened her eyes, Gavin had one baby and the nurse the other. Carefully, they each tucked a snugly wrapped infant into Cassidy's arms. The nurse excused herself.

Gavin pulled up a chair beside the bed and sat down. "Have you ever seen two more perfect infants?" He was rumpled and fatigued, but he beamed. They had made the joint decision *not* to find out the sex of the twins ahead of time.

"We still have to pick names," she said. "And our list is growing instead of shrinking."

"How about Elvis for the boy?"

"I am *not* naming my son Elvis," she said firmly, looking at Gavin's face to make sure he was kidding.

"Then what?"

"I was thinking Lola for my mother and Reggie for your dad."

"I thought you wanted unusual names, something that stands out."

"I changed my mind," she said, trying to imagine what it was going to be like when two babies toddled around the house.

"Well, I like it," Gavin said firmly. "I'm going to fill out the birth certificates before you change your mind again."

Cassidy's heart swelled as she looked from the pink-capped head to the blue-capped one. "I can't believe we did it," she said. "It's all over."

Gavin laughed out loud, wincing when the babies scrunched up their noses. "No," he whispered, stroking her elbow as he stood and carefully leaned over to kiss her. "It's only begun, Cass. It's only begun."

* * * * *

MILLS & BOON®
Hardback – April 2015

ROMANCE

The Billionaire's Bridal Bargain	Lynne Graham
At the Brazilian's Command	Susan Stephens
Carrying the Greek's Heir	Sharon Kendrick
The Sheikh's Princess Bride	Annie West
His Diamond of Convenience	Maisey Yates
Olivero's Outrageous Proposal	Kate Walker
The Italian's Deal for I Do	Jennifer Hayward
Virgin's Sweet Rebellion	Kate Hewitt
The Millionaire and the Maid	Michelle Douglas
Expecting the Earl's Baby	Jessica Gilmore
Best Man for the Bridesmaid	Jennifer Faye
It Started at a Wedding...	Kate Hardy
Just One Night?	Carol Marinelli
Meant-To-Be Family	Marion Lennox
The Soldier She Could Never Forget	Tina Beckett
The Doctor's Redemption	Susan Carlisle
Wanted: Parents for a Baby!	Laura Iding
His Perfect Bride?	Louisa Heaton
Twins on the Way	Janice Maynard
The Nanny Plan	Sarah M. Anderson

MILLS & BOON®
Large Print – April 2015

ROMANCE

Taken Over by the Billionaire	Miranda L
Christmas in Da Conti's Bed	Sharon Kendri
His for Revenge	Caitlin Crev
A Rule Worth Breaking	Maggie C
What The Greek Wants Most	Maya Bla
The Magnate's Manifesto	Jennifer Haywa
To Claim His Heir by Christmas	Victoria Park
Snowbound Surprise for the Billionaire	Michelle Dougl
Christmas Where They Belong	Marion Lenn
Meet Me Under the Mistletoe	Cara Col
A Diamond in Her Stocking	Kandy Shephe

HISTORICAL

Strangers at the Altar	Marguerite Ka
Captured Countess	Ann Lethbrid
The Marquis's Awakening	Elizabeth Beac
Innocent's Champion	Meriel Ful
A Captain and a Rogue	Liz Tyr

MEDICAL

It Started with No Strings...	Kate Har
One More Night with Her Desert Prince...	Jennifer Tay
Flirting with Dr Off-Limits	Robin Gian
From Fling to Forever	Avril Tremay
Dare She Date Again?	Amy Rutt
The Surgeon's Christmas Wish	Annie O'N

MILLS & BOON®
Hardback – May 2015

ROMANCE

e Sheikh's Secret Babies	Lynne Graham
e Sins of Sebastian Rey-Defoe	Kim Lawrence
Her Boss's Pleasure	Cathy Williams
aptive of Kadar	Trish Morey
e Marakaios Marriage	Kate Hewitt
aving Her Enemy's Touch	Rachael Thomas
e Greek's Pregnant Bride	Michelle Smart
reek's Last Redemption	Caitlin Crews
e Pregnancy Secret	Cara Colter
Bride for the Runaway Groom	Scarlet Wilson
e Wedding Planner and the CEO	Alison Roberts
und by a Baby Bump	Ellie Darkins
ways the Midwife	Alison Roberts
idwife's Baby Bump	Susanne Hampton
Kiss to Melt Her Heart	Emily Forbes
mpted by Her Italian Surgeon	Louisa George
aring to Date Her Ex	Annie Claydon
e One Man to Heal Her	Meredith Webber
e Sheikh's Pregnancy Proposal	Fiona Brand
nding Her Boss's Business	Janice Maynard

MILLS & BOON®
Large Print – May 2015

ROMANCE

The Secret His Mistress Carried	Lynne Graham
Nine Months to Redeem Him	Jennie Lucas
Fonseca's Fury	Abby Green
The Russian's Ultimatum	Michelle Smart
To Sin with the Tycoon	Cathy Williams
The Last Heir of Monterrato	Andie Brock
Inherited by Her Enemy	Sara Craven
Taming the French Tycoon	Rebecca Winters
His Very Convenient Bride	Sophie Pembroke
The Heir's Unexpected Return	Jackie Braun
The Prince She Never Forgot	Scarlet Wilson

HISTORICAL

Marriage Made in Money	Sophia James
Chosen by the Lieutenant	Anne Herries
Playing the Rake's Game	Bronwyn Scott
Caught in Scandal's Storm	Helen Dickson
Bride for a Knight	Margaret Moore

MEDICAL

Playing the Playboy's Sweetheart	Carol Marinelli
Unwrapping Her Italian Doc	Carol Marinelli
A Doctor by Day...	Emily Forbes
Tamed by the Renegade	Emily Forbes
A Little Christmas Magic	Alison Roberts
Christmas with the Maverick Millionaire	Scarlet Wilson